Brad's Universe

by
Mary Woodbury

ORCA BOOK PUBLISHERS

Canadian Cataloguing in Publication Data
Woodbury, Mary, 1935 –
Brad's universe

ISBN 1-55143-120-3

I. Title.
PS8595.O644B73 1998   jC813'.54   C97-911118-8   PZ7.W8598Br 1998

Library of Congress Catalog Card Number: 97-81081

Orca Book Publishers gratefully acknowledges the support of our publishing programs provided by the following agencies: the Department of Canadian Heritage, The Canada Council for the Arts, and the British Columbia Ministry Arts Council.

Cover design by Christine Toller
Cover illustration by Ron Lightburn
Printed and bound in Canada

Orca Book Publishers
PO Box 5626, Station B
Victoria, BC Canada
V8R 6S4

Orca Book Publishers
PO Box 468
Custer, WA   USA
98240-0468

00 99 98   5 4 3 2 1

Dedicated to
Jon Mortensen (August 24, 1963 – July 3, 1997),
Timothy J. Anderson,
and my husband, Clair Woodbury,
who each in their own way
contributed their stories
to this fictional book.

☆

Contents

1. THE HOMECOMING

BRAD GREAVES JOGGED to the garage. His hands fumbled as he unlocked his mountain bike with its homemade paper cart attached. He wheeled down the driveway past the carragana hedge and the old willow that crowded the laneway, past bags of potting soil, fertilizer and sand, and his mother's garden tools leaning against the side door. The too rich smell of humus threatened to overpower him like the dark shadows in his head.

Flower beds lined the walk, clustered around a giant rockery in the center of the front lawn. Sweat on Brad's big hands made the handle grips of the bicycle slippery. Tangled blondish hair hung over his broad forehead. His square jaw was set so hard his teeth ached. His steely blue eyes glinted with the fierceness of a falcon. The voices in his head beat large muscular wings. He could still hear his mother's sharp tones.

I don't want you asking your father a lot of questions when he gets home. Kids ask too many questions ... sometimes it's better not to know ... better to keep quiet. Then she had gone, her sturdy body trailing scarves and beads, fluttering hands patting her graying hair and searching for car keys and waving goodbye. The car had sputtered as if it was reluctant to leave the driveway.

Brad forced his mind to think about something solid, something dependable, secure. He had been reading about the nervous system as he tried to get to sleep last night, but he couldn't remember much. Images of his long-absent father's face had floated between his eyes and the anatomy book.

Brad arched over his bike like an Olympic cyclist and pedalled fast. He had to get to the paper drop before Buckles dumped his bundle or stole a couple of inserts. Today of all days he didn't want to tangle with Rory Buckholz.

Old man Drum's Irish setter woofed, then loped by, flinging dust clouds from elegant paws. The setter kept Brad company on his rounds.

The September sun rose behind the Camden hills and washed the morning star from view. Brad loved the stars. The night sky over Camden was the best, not like Saskatoon where they had lived last year, Saskatoon with all its street lights, office towers and search lights.

Brad scanned the horizon: two pale green grain elevators, six church steeples, one main street, two traffic lights and one long stucco composite school where he and all the other kids in elementary and junior high went. Brad had friends at school, in Scouts and on his paper route. He had built a good life in the past six months, since he and his mom had moved here. Why did his dad have to come home and change things? He gripped the handlebars so tightly his knuckles throbbed. He took a deep breath, stared down at his hands.

Amazing things, hands. Over twenty bones in the wrist, hand and fingers—eight carpals, six metacarpals, fourteen phalanges in the fingers, two in the thumb and three in each of the fingers. Add the tendons, nerves, arteries, veins, skin and nails and you have one of the great wonders of the world. Brad felt the tension in his jaw relax, the darkness fade as he remembered the facts he had stored in his brain last night. He shook the tightness out of his hands and slackened his grip on the handlebars.

Nicks and gouges decorated the skin and two Band-aids hid his fingers, or should he call them phalanges. Big, awkward hands that used to work better. Take the row of carved dogs in his shop. He'd painted them when he was a little kid of nine. Now that he was fourteen, holding a tiny horsehair brush in giant paws was tricky.

Brad looked up as he turned the corner onto Main Street. Oh, no. Buckles was bent over Brad's paper bundle pulling out the contents.

"Get lost, Buckles." Brad skidded his bike up over the curb to the tumbled newspapers.

Buckles stood up, shoved greasy brown hair away from his bluish face, flexed muscles beneath the black leather jacket with its chrome plated studs, buckles and shiny zippers. Skin-tight black jeans were tucked into high black boots. He danced over like a trained boxer, waving a rolled up paper in Brad's eyes. "En garde, Bradley."

Then he whirled the paper over his head, tossed it in the air, gave a war whoop and raced for his bike.

The newspaper fell on Brad's head, sweeping across his forehead like the dumb branches of the willow that choked the lane by his house. Brad's head ached. He clenched and unclenched his fists, stormed over and pushed his face so close to Buckles he could smell stale cigarette smoke in Buckle's clothes, sweat and dirt from his body. The air stilled.

"Don't mess with my papers anymore, Buckles ... or I'll beat the, beat the ..."

"Listen to the goody-goody guy. Goin' to use bad language, Bradlee-ee? Ya oughtta be ashamed."

Buckles laughed, shook his head and turned away. Brad's arm shot out and he swung Buckles around, grabbed the lapels of the boy's fancy leather jacket. The sharp metal on the collar dug into Brad's palms but he didn't let go, instead he pulled Buckles closer. The kid's breath was deadly, like rancid hamburger. Buckles' arms flailed at his sides, his eyes filled with surprise and panic. With a sudden heave he freed himself from Brad's grip and fell to the ground, landing smack on one of the spilled papers.

"Okay, okay, Brad, I was just jokin'. Hey, can't ya take a joke, buddy?" Buckles scrambled to his feet and took off on his bike towards the railroad tracks, muttering swear words all the way.

Brad stood, fists balled, ready to strike, ready to punch the stuffing out of the kid. He was shaking with anger but there was no one to hit. A drop of blood fell on the gravel. Brad's right palm stung where the metal buckle had scratched it. He wiped his hand on his jeans, gazed up and down the street to see if anyone had seen the near fight.

Buffalo biscuits! He used his friend Kenny's favorite expression. *What's come over me?* Brad rescued the newspapers, stuck them in the cart and wheeled away.

At home he raced upstairs for his schoolbooks, dashing past his mom's cluttered bedroom with its chintz curtains and spread, smelling of lavender perfume and his dad's bare room with the bed freshly made and a bouquet of fresh marigolds on the dresser. Throat tight, hand hurting, Brad stopped in the bathroom to apply another Band-aid.

He leaned down so he could see in the bathroom mirror, squinting blue-gray eyes, twisting full lips. *En garde, Buckles.* His square face shone red. He splashed water over his freckles, combed his thatch of ash blond hair. Noted with disgust that his favorite Rolling Stones t-shirt was tight across his chest. Soon he'd have to shop in the Big and Tall store. Brad didn't mind being big; he just didn't want to be a freak of nature.

He decided to stop by Kenny and Lane's house on his way to school.

☆

Traynor's dog barked as Brad pulled in the driveway; the cat darted for the pansies. Lane Traynor stuck her head out the front door, "Kenny can't find his homework."

Brad wanted suddenly to run after Lane, tell her about Buckles and his dad coming home and the sudden war going on inside himself. Instead he plodded quietly after her into the warm, toast-and-coffee-smelling kitchen.

"Toast and jam, Bradley?" Anna Traynor motioned to Kenny's empty place at the table. "Milk?"

Brad downed a glassful.

Grant Traynor glanced over the top of his newspaper. "Papers late? Any problems?"

"No, sir." He grinned, thinking about Buckles sprawled on the ground, staring up at him with a dazed look in his eyes. The kid hadn't been that big after all. Kind of scrawny.

"Mom, I can't find my homework. I'm going to be toast,"

Kenny's voice filled the stairwell. "I hate detentions."

"Hurry, Kenny," Brad said as he scooped another piece of toast from the pile in the center of the table, lathered it with margarine and grape jelly. "You should know what you are like by now."

"I suppose your stuff is always tucked neatly in your backpack, eh, bozobreath?" Kenny punched his arm. "Seems to me you lost track of your last math assignment."

"Try the coffee table." Mrs. Traynor pulled on a bright red bush jacket. A few pine needles fell to the floor and a trace of woodsy smell floated around the kitchen. Her dark wavy hair shone, her hazel eyes danced, her smooth fair skin glistened from soap, and a dash of lipstick brightened her face. She bent and kissed the top of her husband's head, just where he was going bald. "Love you. I've a meeting with all the park rangers this afternoon so I could be late."

"Who's going to take me to swimming lessons?" Lane came out of the downstairs bathroom. Her short black hair had been brushed but still waved and wandered over her forehead. Her black eyebrows were bushy and nearly met in the middle. The other kids teased her about it, called her Neanderthal, but Brad thought it gave her a fierce and bold look that he liked.

"Can you see out?" Her mother pushed the shiny black mop away from Lane's temples and planted a kiss. "You'll have to take yourself."

"I'm a neglected child. Nobody loves me."

"That's not funny," Brad said. He bit his lip. Stupid remark, Brad. These were his only friends. Hard to believe they were twins, they were such absolute opposites.

"What's eating you?" Lane tossed a worn paperback at him.

Brad ducked, bent and picked up the murder mystery

she was currently reading. He handed it back without saying a word. Lane always poked into his life.

"Found it, under Lane's candy wrappers. Buffalo chips." Kenny grabbed his notebook. He was wearing bulky gray sweats and a Beatles t-shirt like his sister's. His straight black hair was combed back flat from his thin face with its narrow nose. Bony hands waved the homework aloft. Kenny gave his mom a hug and turned to face Brad.

"What's up?"

"Well, I've got some news for you." Brad's voice cracked on the last three words, as if he was having a struggle getting the words out. His voice was changing but sometimes it sounded dumb.

"So tell us?" Lane flicked her hair out of her eyes.

"Yeah! Spill the beans, as my dad would say." Kenny tried to buckle his bag.

"Wait until we get outside. It's kind of private."

"You mean there is something we don't know about you? Wow, I can hardly wait." Lane mocked surprise. Mornings she was usually giggly. Kenny was moody.

The three kids made their way to the front door, past the leaping dog and the prancing cat. Lane squeezed through the door. Brad and Kenny followed her.

They climbed on their bikes and wheeled towards school.

Brad frowned, and squinted once or twice. He wanted to tell Lane about his dad coming back from the hospital, the one that his mom said didn't allow kids under sixteen to visit. It was a mental hospital and his dad had been there for a year. He wanted to tell Lane, but at the same time he didn't want to tell. Would the Traynors still be his friends if they thought his dad was, well, you know, sick in the head? He plunged ahead.

"The good news is I don't think Buckles is going to bother me anymore."

"That bully," said Lane.

"He's a meatball." Kenny nursed his right arm. Only yesterday it had been twisted by Buckles during gym. "Tell all, oh great Gorgonzola."

Brad told them about the near-fight, showed them his wounded hand. They turned the corner by the school and walked to the bike racks.

"I need to shoot baskets," Kenny said, "sore arm or not. How about it, Brad? You're tall enough to be a forward, even against the Senior High. Half your jeans are high-waters, you dork. When are you going to stop growing, eh? You could end up being the biggest mozza on the team in a couple of years."

"Will not." Brad glanced down at his legs. He could see his socks. Shoot. He'd have to get Mom to buy the next bigger size jeans.

"What's the other news?" Lane asked. "You said you had bad news."

"No, he didn't," Kenny said.

"Yes, well, it's not important, you probably don't want to know. I mean, it doesn't change anything, at least I hope it won't." Brad wanted to run suddenly. Why did he say anything at all? Did they really need to know? It's hard to explain a six-foot man and a noisy piano without saying something.

"Spit it out," Kenny giggled.

"My dad's coming home tonight."

Lane lifted her head from locking her bike, "I thought he was gone, divorced or dead. You never talk about him. Why? Did he run away or something? You'll have to say more than that, Brad."

"It's family stuff." Brad shook himself as if he were coming out of a swimming pool. "I'm not sure how to …" He felt a blush spread to the roots of his hair. Lane studied his face and nodded.

"I didn't know you had a father!" Kenny's eyes were wide. "Where's he been?"

"Oh, shut up Kenny." Lane walked toward the cluster of girls by the back door.

"He's been away," Brad said."Okay?"

Kenny blushed.

Brad picked up books and homework, scuffed the right toe of his sneakers in the dirt. He strode past Kenny, past the yellow school bus with the farm and acreage kids climbing off chattering and shoving each other.

"Buffalo biscuits." Shaking his head in amazement, Kenny ran to catch up.

School was uneventful. Kenny told some of the others about the near-fight between Brad and Buckles, and Buckles and his buddies kept making snide comments about Brad when he passed them in the halls. Brad spent the day in a fog thinking about his dad, who dropped in and out of his life like a visiting comet—or was he a meteor ready to crash? Tall, dark with buggy eyes and baggy trousers, his father had hands like a skeleton, skin the color of parchment. His fingers were always moving quickly, over piano or organ keys, running through long salt and pepper hair or pressing the creases of his pants, caressing his chin or wetting the tips to flatten unruly eyebrows. Would he have changed at all? Mostly Brad remembered his father as being distant, more distant than the stars. Only his music was close and warm.

When Brad got home he peeled the potatoes and put the roast in the oven. His mom had left a list of chores: put on the supper, water the plants, empty wastebaskets, clean your room.

The fern in the music room—the one beside the silent organ—needed fertilizer. He added three drops. The baby grand smelled of lemon wax. Some baby, actually it was a boudoir grand and it took up half of the room. When his father was home, he and the piano seemed to fill the house to overflowing. Big man, big sounds. A mixture of wonderful music and a demanding voice. It was not always an easy thing to be a little kid in a house full of music and his dad. Brad remembered his father playing Rachmaninoff, a rich, warm piece that Brad loved. His father had played it for his favorite students. The bigger boys clustered around the piano listening, and Brad had sat close to the piano humming along with the music, enjoying the rich rhythm and melody. Suddenly he had been sent to the living room with his mother, to play with Lego blocks.

"He's very distracting," his father had said after the boys had left. "The child makes noise, Una. He doesn't appreciate music yet." But Brad had loved that music, he really had.

After that, Brad had played in his mother's sewing room whenever his father had a little gathering. No room for a little boy back then. Would there be any room for a big boy? Part of Brad wanted his father to come home and discover he had a big boy now, not a little kid. Maybe they could start over. He let his large hand slide over the shiny black surface of the piano. For a moment traces of his damp finger prints showed and then nothing, nothing but the gloss of the polished wood.

The first time his dad left, Brad had been maybe six or seven. He'd come home from school and found his mother crying. Everything seemed cloudy, dark as a moonless night. They must have been living somewhere damp because Brad could smell mildew and rain, and wet rubber boots. They had moved. Brad ran up against a wall of fog in his memory. He wiped sweaty palms on his knees and let his mind skip forward to when his father had come back. They had chicken and dumplings for supper. The dumplings were soggy. His dad had tuned the piano and yelled at Brad to pick up his toys, while his mom had stood between the two of them explaining in a quiet voice, explaining how to be nice to each other. His father's huge eyes had gone weird, like marbles rolling up into his head. Brad had run outside.

Brad left the watering can by the philodendron on the landing and went into his room. It was plant-free. He pulled out his homework assignment, a photocopied picture of a tree with boxes. The family tree.

"Get your parents to help you fill it out," Mrs. Peebles had said in her smooth, sophisticated voice. "Tell a story about your family history." Brad scratched his head. He didn't have any family history, not that he'd ever heard. He'd ask mom about it, but there was some mystery about mom and her family. He knew what she'd say. She'd say, "Leave sleeping dogs lie."

Maybe he could borrow some of the Traynors' relatives; they had oodles of them, some buried in a pioneer graveyard near Red Deer. The Scouts had had a picnic on the grass there, and Brad had eaten six tuna sandwiches and three pieces of chocolate cake.

Brad pulled hockey cards out of his pocket, but they slipped through his broad fingers and fell to the floor. He picked them up. Life felt all jumbled up like those cards. He liked life to go smoothly so he could concentrate on learning stuff. If he didn't learn enough, he'd never be good at anything. If he became really good at something, then he would know he deserved to be here on this planet. Otherwise, a guy might as well leave. Learn or leave, the dark inside his head sneered.

"Live and learn," his Scoutmaster, Lane and Kenny's dad, would say. "Live and learn." Grant Traynor was a great bear of a man who loved kids, but his idea of talking about things usually came with a lot of sayings attached.

A car door banged. Brad gulped, feeling his Adam's apple jiggling in his throat. He shoved the hockey cards in a deep dark pocket in his jeans, pushed his fingers through his hair and ran downstairs.

☆

"Anybody home?" His mother swung the screen door wide, and stood there grinning, her lopsided smile emphasizing the permanently-sad frozen half of her face. Her angel wisp hair blew in the breeze, her green scarf threatened to fall to the floor. She was holding the door open so the tall man carrying a suitcase could come in. "We're here."

Brad blushed and turned away, spotted the potatoes sitting on the counter. "I forgot to put the potatoes around the roast. I'll boil them."

"Say hello to your father, Brad." His mother's voice was louder, sharper than usual. She rushed to the sink to run water into a saucepan. Brad and she nearly collided. Her hand shook as she reached for the faucet. Desmond Greaves, on the opposite side of the room, dropped a beat-up suitcase by the nearest chair. His protruding eyes searched Brad's face.

"Still favor your mother's family, I see. Big feet and hands, and a broad chest like a farmer." He smiled and held out his hand.

Brad shook it. He was startled. Desmond's hand was not any larger than his now, thinner but not any bigger. Brad was nearly as tall as his dad, too. A strange feeling of power surged through Brad, then raced away. He let go of his father's hand. Desmond's fingers were long and bony and cold like some ghostly skeleton.

His father looked paler and skinnier than Brad remembered. Desmond's rich voice and his spicy after-shave filled the neat kitchen. Brad's mouth went dry.

"Mom, where do we come from—Vancouver, Winnipeg—where?" Brad moved toward his mother. "I need to know for school."

His mother frowned. She shook her head violently. "Not now," she whispered. "How about a tour of the house, Des?" She reached for Desmond's hand and pulled him through the living room into the music room. "See how Bradley and I have set this up for you, Desmond dear."

Brad stirred salt into the boiling potatoes and muttered, "I didn't do anything, mom. You did the room." You fussed over every sheet of music, ream of staff paper, folder of concertos, sheaf of diplomas, he thought to himself.

Steam from the vegetables fogged his glasses. He took them off and wiped them with a tissue from the top of the refrigerator. Brad poured water into tumblers and checked the roast, folded napkins and put them beside the plates. He studied his hands. They were so different from his dad's hands; they were farmer's hands as he had said. Why did that sound like a dirty thing? The farmers around Camden worked hard, were prosperous. They knew what they were doing. He pushed his hands deep in his pockets, past the hockey cards, past the house keys and the change, pressing the seams at the bottom, feeling traces of lint and thread.

A dissonant chord echoed from the music room, "Piano's out of tune." Minutes later a keyboard version of Vivaldi's *Four Seasons* filled the house. Brad's mother clapped.

"I sure missed this," Desmond said as the last chord died away.

Brad had missed the music, too. His father's music was like a fourth presence in the house. For more than a year there had been Brad and his mom and the stillness. Once more there was the whole family and the music and something else, some shadow that crowded the corners of each room.

"The piano at That Place was always out of tune." His father's voice continued. "The hammer for the bottom G was missing."

Brad stuck giant hands into bright blue oven mitts and pulled the roast leg of lamb from the oven. It sizzled as he transferred it to the platter and sharpened the carving knife. Suddenly he could see himself in the next few years gaining control over his hands, and then his head, and a small niggling voice with a vision of Lane and the Traynor's house behind it whispered—heart. What a silly kid to think always in threes! He would leave the heart out of it. He would start with his hands. Brad grinned at how nice the roast looked as he carved thick, juicy slices. While his dad had been away, he had been in charge of this job. He wasn't ready to hand it back. When he had finished and the smell of steaming lamb filled the kitchen, he called out.

"Supper's ready."

The Greaves family sat down to their first meal together

after more than a year. As Brad buttered his roll and ate it, he couldn't help feeling a little hopeful. Maybe this time …

"Camden has a little mall with a music store," Mrs. Greaves said. "Maybe you could work …"

"Pass the mint sauce." Desmond chewed loudly, quickly, as if worried someone might take food from his plate.

"I'm in Scouts …" Brad started to say.

"There's no one left to play piano in That Place. Everyone liked to sing." Desmond Greaves scooped potatoes into his mouth. "Even the guards, I mean, the …"

"Gardeners, Desmond," Brad's mom leapt into the conversation, "singing gardeners, you say … Let's not talk about it, you're home now. That's what matters, isn't that right, Brad? Your dad's home, that's what matters." Her fingers patted the curls at the nape of her neck. Her voice had risen sharply.

Brad swallowed the last of his roll soaked in gravy from the roast. "I've got homework." The kitchen had become too small for the three of them.

He escaped to his room, moving restlessly among his things, flipping open the anatomy book and then closing it, adjusting the hanging model, pulling the cord on the vertical blinds to let in the fading light. Wide patio doors overlooked the fields behind Camden and the wide prairie, the endless Alberta sky. Brad slid the glass door open and escaped onto the balcony. An early moon hovered near the eastern edge of the horizon. He filled his lungs with cool, fresh air. Here was Brad's own private view of the universe, an expanding, breathtaking universe full of honest straightforward mysteries that begged to be understood. He could spend a lifetime exploring those mysteries. Better than TV or books or mashed potatoes and gravy. So much to see, so much to learn, so much to master.

"Nice house, Una," his father's voice floated up from the garden. "But it seems like a silly little town, perched on the edge of nowhere. Not very inspiring, eh? I prefer the city." His voice dropped. "It's good to be home. I need you, Una …" The two adults whispered back and forth. Brad could not hear the words.

He gripped the railing with broad hands and leaned towards the moon. The darkness outside was so friendly, the night sky so ordered. Didn't his father or mother see what he saw? His foot, propped on the base of the wooden railing around the balcony, slipped and landed on the porch floor with a bang.

"Is that you, Bradley, dear?" His mother asked.

"You better get inside. Are you wearing a jacket?" His father's voice was sharp as scissors. "You'll catch a cold. Stupid kid."

The darkness in Brad's head exploded.

2. It's only a game

THE FAMILY TREE assignment sat on Brad's desk for several weeks. Every time he brought up the subject his mom said she was too busy or going out to sell a farm. He picked it up once more and stared at it, shook his head. What was he going to do?

Downstairs his father was teaching Mrs. Chan. All his father's students were grownups. Brad's mother sat in the corner of the music room, listening to the music, nodding in time to the metronome. Before his dad came back, Brad and his mom would have made supper together, done the dishes, read in the living room or watched TV. He missed that. Brad cracked his knuckles and threw a crumpled piece of paper at the wastebasket. It missed, too.

He picked up the paper and tossed it again, his head hitting the "Next Generation" *Enterprise* model. It swung back and forth in time with the strains of a Bach exercise. It should swing all the time. What if he brought the old fan from the basement, attached a socket to the ceiling light and rigged an extension to the wall plug that was hooked to the light switch? When he turned on the light the fan would blow on the *Enterprise* and it would move in the breeze.

Brad ran down to the basement, fished through a drawer of light switches, spare parts and cords until he had all the pieces he needed, raced up the stairs and into his room. He set to work. If he hurried he'd get it finished before it was time to leave for Scouts.

He was in the midst of hammering clamps into the wall to carry the extension cord to the base plug when his father flung open the door.

"Mother, can't you do anything about this boy?" He glared at Brad, raised his right hand. Brad backed away. His mother came to the door, put a restraining hand on Desmond's arm. The two of them filled the doorframe.

"He's just a boy," she said quietly. A nerve twitched in her cheek. "You should remember ..."

Brad's hands hung loose at his sides. The cords of his father's neck stretched taut like steel cables on a bridge, his large brown eyes stuck out. His skin was pale, as if it hadn't been exposed to the sun for years. He smelled musty like the gray wool blankets in the back of the linen closet.

"When I was a boy, my father beat me. I've never laid a finger on you. Never." His father shuddered. "In That Place people who didn't behave were isolated."

Brad's head dropped to his chest. The tension in the room was palpable. It would be easier if his dad hit him. He stared at the nubby carpet. His father left. In the hallway Desmond began talking gently to Mrs. Chan, "Let's hear that exercise again."

The woman said something.

"You have a very light touch."

Mrs. Chan laughed happily.

"All my students have developed a light touch. It's one of my specialties."

"Oh, thank you, Mr. Greaves, you are too kind." The music room door closed. The sounds of Bach continued.

His mother was talking to him. Brad tried to concentrate on the words, but his mind kept running away, like a frightened deer. He measured the carpet. The mat by the door must be a meter long by about ninety centimeters. How did they get the weave so tight? Did they use robots on the looms instead of people for the boring work? Thinking about real things, about the way things were made, was safe. There were answers to those questions, answers in books, on the Internet or on science programs on TV. It was not safe to think too much about people. That's when the darkness invaded.

"He's still getting used to living with us, working ..." his mother was saying. "Give him time, Brad." Her eyes pleaded, silently searching his face for clues to how he felt. He turned his head away. "You have always been a good boy. You are just at an awkward age, I guess."

A lightning flash of anger scorched Brad's brain. I'm not the awkward one here. Dad is, he wanted to shout. His watch beeped. "Scouts." Brad escaped across the carpet and down the stairs on tiptoe past his mother's plants. The thick smell of geraniums and gloxinias choked him. The tick of the metronome, the soft, sad eyes of his mother and the sound of his father speaking encouragingly to Mrs. Chan made him long for the open air, away from this little house that felt too crowded, too dark.

Brad leapt on his bike and raced to the church hall, not stopping for Kenny or Lane, feeling the wind wash over his face, his head bent slightly to keep the fine dust from the road out of his eyes. Drum's Irish Setter broke through the bushes and ran beside him for several blocks. The dog breathed heavily and his coat rippled and shimmered in the moonglow and streetlights. He glanced up at Brad with something close to a doggy smile. He had gray whiskers on his chin, much like Old Drum's. They were quite the pair, the old man and his dog. Brad saw one or both of them every day. Like the moon and stars they were dependable. Brad's racing heart slowed, his hands on the handlebars relaxed.

The moon looked huge close to the horizon, an optical illusion of course. The largest satellite, compared to its planet, in the solar system. Other planets have more moons but most are smaller. Earth's moon, that bright disc, was 2,160 miles in diameter and circled 238,000 miles or so away, on an elliptical orbit. It was very old, about 1½ billion years old. That was too old to imagine. Brad wanted to live to be an old man, older than Mr. Drum, so he could learn all he wanted, so he could do something, do something that would make a difference.

Just outside the Anglican church Kenny and Lane caught up to him.

"What's that ticking on your bike?" Kenny asked. "Sounds like a bomb."

"It's a homemade pedometer, so I can keep track of distance, how far I've been, you know."

"How?" Kenny locked his bike in the rack by the church hall door. "Wonder who's got the key. Hope Dad has, we don't want to have the meeting outside."

"Worrywart," Lane joined Brad. "Are you going to explain?" She bent and studied the piece of plastic attached to the spoke on his front wheel. "It clicks against the cross piece once every revolution, right? And you have measured the circumference of the wheel."

"It is eighty-three centimeters," Brad said. "A hundred and twenty-two klicks and I know I've gone 100 meters. It's

500 meters from my place to your place. I cycle five kilometers to do my paper route. I counted. Next, I'll invent an electronic gizmo to count for me."

"Awesome." Kenny pummeled Brad's back. "Do you think something has happened to the caretaker? Should we get a key from the priest? It is getting cold out here. We don't want to catch colds. Have to keep sharp for that socials test tomorrow. Do you think one of us should go and phone?"

Lane and Brad glanced at each other over Kenny's frown, and shook their heads simultaneously: No!

Matt Peebles, Kenny and Lane's cousin, came strolling down the street, shoving handfuls of potato chips into his open mouth. He had a sturdy boxcar body and didn't look at all like his sophisticated slim mother, the Social Studies teacher. Two other guys wheeled up.

"Where's Ashley?" Matt asked. Brad figured he had a crush on Ashley Sargent, Lane's best friend.

"She's babysitting for the priest and his wife. They've gone on a heavy date into Edmonton to the opera." Lane squinted. Lane and Ashley had been friends since first grade. Brad had moved too often to bother with friends before this. He still wasn't sure what friends were for, or how you kept them. But he wanted to figure it out because the Traynors were special people, all of them.

The 2nd Scout Troop that met in the hall Thursday nights came walking down the street with their leader, Trevor, who was sporting a skimpy new beard. Brad felt his muscles tighten. Kenny had said Trevor was too aggressive for his dad's liking. Brad watched the guy stalking down the street, kind of like Buckles, only more confident. He didn't like the air of superiority that hung around the man's shoulders. He didn't like anyone who didn't treat the Traynors with respect.

"We've been to the fire hall," one of Trevor's Scouts shouted.

Grant Traynor, dressed in his Scoutmaster uniform, pulled up in the rusty brown Honda the family used for errands or camping.

Trevor unlocked the wide church door and his gang of kids plunged into the mothball-and-lemon-wax-smelling hall. St. Alban's had high ceiling and wooden rafters. The walls were decorated with tattered attendance charts covered with silver stars, a terrible oil painting of Jesus holding a lantern, and a slightly crooked basketball hoop with its net drooping. The hall wasn't long enough for a real basketball game.

"How about a game of floor hockey before my boys go home?" Trevor said. "Five against six isn't bad." His six stood waiting, wriggling, punching each other, scuffling amongst themselves.

"It's even steven," Grant Traynor stared at his Scouts hanging their coats on nails by the door, changing into indoor shoes, old worn sneakers without mud or gravel. "The Camden 1st Scouts against the Camden 2nd."

"We don't play girls," a skinny boy shouted.

Grant straightened from tying his runners. He tucked his sagging tummy in, hitched his trousers up. His bristly chin squared, hardened.

"Lane is a Scout. If you are challenging us to a game, then she's included." Fire shone in his eyes and he glared at Trevor, so pimply and narrow-shouldered.

"Girls can't be Scouts," one boy piped up.

Brad wrinkled his forehead. "They can be Venturers."

Kenny whispered, "We've been waiting for this. Trevor and Dad used to do Scouts together, but when the girls' troop folded, Lane said she wanted to join Scouts. Dad said great. Trevor didn't like it. So he quit. Started his own group."

"What's his problem?" Brad glanced at Lane. Her face was red as a beet, her shoulders stiff, her fists clenched.

"Okay," Trevor said. "But don't blame us if she gets hurt."

"A bunch of wimps and sissies," one kid hissed as he and a tubby guy set up the goals. The mouthy kid nodded toward Brad, "Hey, doesn't your Dad teach piano? Only sucks play piano."

Brad whipped around from digging the sticks out of the closet. His face flamed. Lane handed him a pile of chopped-off hockey sticks. "They aren't worth it, Brad, they're just a bunch of baby machos."

Brad was goalie first. Matt, Lane, Kenny and the other Scouts lined up. Trevor's crew lined up opposite. Grant leaned against the wall, chewing on a toothpick, hands in his pockets, faking casual interest. Trevor held the whistle.

By the end of first period the score was one to one. Grant's Scouts had the advantage with their size, but Trevor's crew were smaller and more agile. Brad was on defense and Lane was in goal. Kenny scored a big one to make it two to one.

Trevor's Scouts surged down the gym sliding the puck back and forth in a good pattern. Most of them were seasoned hockey players and skated regularly at the Camden rink. What with moving around, Brad had never learned to skate until recently, let alone play any game with an eye to strategy. He definitely felt at a disadvantage. He bit his lip.

Brad shadowed the biggest kid. Just as they got near the goal Brad slipped on the greasy floor and the guy fired the puck. Lane made a great save by dropping to her knees. Another kid took the rebound and slammed the puck toward the goal. It whistled through the air.

Brad leaped across two players and sprawled in front of

the goal. The rubber ring thwacked his leg full force.

"Umph! I did it. I blocked it!" Brad shouted with glee.

Lane leaned over to help Brad up. Trevor called the face-off between Kenny and the tubby kid.

"Brad, relax," Lane whispered. "It's just a game."

Brad blinked sweat out of his eyes and stood behind Kenny, ready for the toss. If he couldn't control his temper, he should leave Scouts. He couldn't guarantee how he was going to behave. He kept getting carried away. It wasn't cool.

"It's just a game, just a game," he repeated to himself.

3. BINOCULARS

SATURDAY'S PAPERS WERE late. Brad hung around waiting, tossing rocks at old Drum's garage door until Drum yelled at him to stop. Brad leaped on his bike and raced home without waiting for the *Journal* truck.

As he skidded into the space between the weeping willow and his mother's gardening tools, he could hear his folks bickering, his dad's voice loud, his mother's soft and insistent. He wanted to cover his ears; it reminded him of woodpeckers banging their beaks on tin.

"You've let that boy take over the house, mother. His tools in the basement, his books in the sitting room, his stuff spread all over the biggest bedroom in the place. Weren't you planning on me coming home?"

"Brad's a good boy, he's good at school. He studies in his room, so he needs more space." His mother's voice was pleading. "Live and let live."

"Fine for you, but how am I supposed to live, what with your plants and that boy's junk?"

"He needs room for his inventions, his workshop." Brad's mom went on. "He's very quiet, really, when he's working on something."

"Stick up for him, go ahead. What about me?" Desmond Greaves' voice lowered. "I was the bright young man who rescued you from a dull life, remember? I was the child prodigy, wasn't I? I could play Liszt when I was nine, played at the conservatory when I was twelve. Brad can't play a kazoo."

"Of course, dear, of course," Brad's mom whispered. "I don't want my two boys jealous of each other, do I?"

"Jealous, are you kidding," his father shouted. "Why would I be jealous?"

Brad let his bike handle bang against the outside wall. He kicked the bottom step.

"Is that you, Bradley, dear?" his mother's voice asked cheerily. "Want some orange juice? An apple Danish?"

Brad closed his eyes and opened them, once, twice, to see if the anger would go away. He couldn't very well blow up about a conversation he had overheard. Besides, his dad wasn't Buckles; he couldn't scare him. Why, oh why had Dad come home?

He pushed past his father. His mother clucked, circling the kitchen, filling tumblers with juice and putting a plate with microwaved buns on the table. His mother handled all difficulties with food or by fussing around. Brad's head throbbed. He went to the bathroom, tossed water on his flushed face and came back, threw himself into the chair. One of the rungs popped.

"A bloody savage." His father flung the hair from his eyes and stirred another teaspoon of sugar into his coffee. "You'll have to move your junk from the basement. I need more space. Don't plan on doing anything with your little friends this afternoon."

Brad gulped his juice, grabbed the chair he'd been sitting on and leaned it against the wall. "I'll fix this when I get back."

His mother's face looked puzzled.

"The papers were late. I have to deliver them." He picked up the rung and set it carefully on top of the oak chair and left his father sitting at the table, his mother hesitating between the kitchen sink and the stove. "More coffee, Desmond? Another Danish?"

"I'll be back in an hour." Anger clogged Brad's breathing. "I'll move my own stuff ... out to the shed ... so it's not in your way."

His father stared through the screen at him, then turned to Una May. "Like the camel in the nomad's tent, Una. You have to make sure they know who's in charge."

As Brad wheeled away, the tightness in his throat moved to his ears. "I'm not a camel, I'm a kid," he muttered. A hawk shrieked as it dived. Brad scanned the horizon; he couldn't spot the bird, but he could see the moon fading, tilted like a cup pouring blue sky and clouds towards the earth. It filled his chest with moon dust, gave him space to breath, to think, to stretch his mind to the farthest corner of the solar system.

Last night he'd watched the movie *Moonstruck* on video over at the Traynors'. The moon had a magic for him, too. Maybe it was just reflected light but it warmed him. If he had been up at midnight he could have seen the half moon nearly upright. Out by twelve degrees because the earth, the earth was tilted that much always. Some book would explain to him in detail just how and why it worked that way.

The papers had finally arrived. Brad tossed the bundle onto his cart and whistled the "Star Trek" series theme as he delivered them.

☆

The fall sun scorched the horizon, turning the threshed wheat fields pale gold like corn syrup. Sweat ran into Brad's eyes as he pulled into the laneway. The kitchen was spotless and empty. Bangs and thumps from the dark and dusty basement drew him down the steep steps with their worn rubber treads.

"Here's my trophy from the Kiwanis Festival 1959, top marks piano under sixteen. Una May, you should have seen me. But in '59 you were ..."

"... already at teacher's college. Remember, I robbed the cradle, marrying you, Des." Both parents laughed. Mrs. Greaves whacked a spider fiercely, turned to her son. "Oh, hi, Brad. We left your stuff."

"People can be so picky about their belongings. They certainly were in That Place." Desmond was polishing a plaque with a rag and Silvo. "I couldn't stand anyone touching my piano when I was a child, especially my little brother. Such a heavy hand."

Brad grabbed a couple of sturdy boxes from the center of the floor and went to his workbench. He packed his tools in the order they were hung. He would remount them in the shed behind the garage, reuse the plywood backing with its traced and painted shapes; hacksaw, hammer, pliers, set square, coping saw, and a plastic gadget with holes for his screwdrivers, files and carving knives.

His mother groaned. She was trying to lift a massive box from the middle shelf of the storage unit. Brad ran to help her, seeing as his dad seemed oblivious.

Brad wiped a layer of dust from the top. "Grandpa Greaves' mementos," it said.

"Packed it myself when the old man died in the nursing home," Desmond whined. "My brother left it for me to do and flew off to his fancy job and family. Typical."

"Where was he?" Brad asked.

"Who? Your grandpa or your uncle?" his mother asked.

"Either one." He had to put something on the family chart. Maybe his relatives were crooks, or crazy.

"I'm supposed to fill out my family tree, Mom. I need help."

His parents stared at each other, as if some conversation was going on telepathically.

"Your father thinks you should forget that assignment, Brad." His mother broke the long silence.

"It's nobody's business," his father went on. "Like the government asking all sorts of personal questions on census forms. Privacy. People should be allowed ..."

"Should I call the teacher?" Brad's mom asked.

"No," Brad nearly shouted. "Just forget it. I'll think of something." The basement felt colder than he remembered. He went back to helping his mother with the box, listening to his father rant about privacy and poking noses into other people's business.

Brad opened the box and unrolled wads of newspaper, peered into plastic sacks.

"Give it to the Goodwill, it's junk. I'll never use it." His father went back to hanging his diplomas on a freshly painted cement wall.

Brad stared at the ancient white and black photograph of a bunch of Boy Scouts with staffs and knee socks and serious-looking leaders. Much more serious than Grant Traynor. Was life more serious back then, or did they think smiling would make them look foolish?

"One of those boys is your Grandpa Greaves," his mother whispered, looking at Desmond's back. "They didn't get along. He was an angry man, couldn't see how gifted Desmond was ... couldn't see anything but himself. Near the end they wouldn't talk to each other. Cut from different bolts of cloth. Fathers and sons seem to have a struggle. Maybe if you had been a girl ..." His mother covered her mouth with her hand as if willing her last words away.

Brad lay the photo aside to study later and unwrapped the clumsiest package of all. It wasn't old or dusty except for a light film on the black molded case.

"Binoculars," Brad whistled the words under his breath. "Big ones, too."

His father turned from adjusting graduation photographs. "The nurse said he ordered them out of the catalogue two weeks before he died. His old ones had dropped on the floor and smashed to smithereens. Ironic, isn't it, Una, he never used them."

"They're 10 by 50 lens," Brad held them to his eyes, focusing on the far wall. It was too close. "Good for stargazing." His mind raced, making plans. He could mount them on a tripod on the balcony. Next time he had a chance to go into the city he would pick up supplies. It would be great. Brad pictured himself out there in the dark and quiet, bundled in a coat, peering through the lens at the whole universe. Alone.

"Fancied himself an astronomer, a man of science." His father was hammering a picture hook into the wall. He struck it so hard it broke. "Only liked marches, the General did. Tough old bird."

Brad put the binoculars back into their case, placed the case and the Scout photo gently on the box of tools for his shop and fled up the stairs.

He cleaned out the shed, scrubbed it down. He made a trip to the basement and rescued his tool box with the binoculars perched on it. Then he gave his workshop a coat of white latex paint. With a small heater, except for the harshest part of winter, this would be great, better than the dark basement, the crowded house. He wouldn't be disturbing anyone. His father wouldn't have to yell.

"Time for lunch, Bradley." His mother stood at the door, admiring his space. "Look how big you are. Who'd ever think you were just a boy?" She held out a box to him. "More like a man."

Brad recognized the box. It was the rest of his grandpa's stuff.

"Your dad told me to throw it out. I thought you might want it." She smiled. "Everything is going to be fine, isn't it? We're lucky people, aren't we? We're a whole family."

Brad nodded. Why ask him? He wasn't in charge of anything. He followed his mother into the house for tomato sandwiches and split pea soup. Her beeper sounded and she went to sell a farm. She seemed to thrive on real estate. More so since Desmond had come back.

His dad came upstairs, washed his hands and the two of them sat eating. The silence between them was thicker than the soup.

The rich taste of fresh tomatoes, mayonnaise and bakery bread reminded Brad of fall lunches in another house, a house before the one they had lived in in Saskatoon. Lunches with his mother and father. A big house with enough room for all of them, an apple tree outside his window, a black cat and hills in the distance, picnics at a lake, an old woman with a big lap and peppermint breath. Fresh tomatoes from a garden, juice dribbling down his chin. Music and laughter and other children. Brad licked a drop of mayonnaise from his finger. The memories faded.

Who were those people he remembered? Where was the

house? Why did the family leave that time?

"You never told me your friend Kenny was such a winner," his father broke the silence. "I was carrying out the papers. Whoever lived here before never cleaned out anything. People are so thoughtless."

"Kenny, what about Kenny?" Brad asked.

"Well, his photo was in the paper. He won top prize in piano in the Kiwanis Festival, and overall prize in the Spring Fair, before you knew him so well. There's a boy any father could be proud of." His father paused, as if he was finished but not quite. "He's good looking too, slight and dark with fine chiseled features."

Brad's teeth clenched. "I'll be a Chief Scout by next summer." He ran from the room.

He fought with the willow branches clogging the laneway, broke a branch and tossed it toward the compost pile, clambered on his bike and rode furiously out of town, down the concession road until he could touch the prairie and the wide, wide sky. His pedometer clicked.

How far was it to the horizon where the Hutterite colony started? Brad began to count the clicks. How many revolutions of the wheel, two, four, six, eight, ten, twelve …? He counted steadily until he was nothing but a dot on the landscape himself.

4. THE PLANETS

BRAD'S MOTHER DROVE the car over to the Traynors' house the next Saturday night. Brad sat in the back. His father drummed his fingers on his knee like he was playing a piano sonata.

"Watch out for that truck, Una."

"I see it, Desmond."

"Go slow. This is a school zone." Brad's dad straightened the rear-view mirror. "Don't crack your knuckles, Bradley, it's impolite."

"It's so nice of the Traynors' to invite us for dinner, don't you think?" Brad's mother patted Desmond's sleeve. "They're nice people, Des."

A tabby cat raced across the street barely missing the front bumper. Two magpies scolded as Mrs. Greaves turned the corner. The chocolate pecan pie in its white cardboard box wrapped with string, from the Camden bakery, slid along the back seat and touched Brad's corduroy pant leg. He was dressed in his church clothes and it felt strange.

"I hope they put their dog and cat out. Did you tell them I had allergies, Bradley? Did you remember that?" Brad's dad combed his hair again, then mopped his lips.

"Una, don't clutch the steering wheel like that. Your

knuckles are white. Relax."

Brad's mother sighed and pulled up in front of the Traynors' house. The garage door was open. The brown Honda had its hood open. A large red tool box lay open beside it. An unruly assortment of bicycles leaned or stood along the walls of the garage. Tools and garden implements were scattered everywhere. The cat lay in the laneway licking its back leg.

"Such chaos." Desmond Greaves folded his hankie neatly and replaced it in the breast pocket of his new Navy blazer.

"They're busy people, Dad."

"It's so nice of them, dear." Una Greaves reached for the pie. "It would be nice to have friends in town, wouldn't it?"

"If I had my way we'd move to the city. I can't find real work. Small towns remind me of days on the farm, remind me of ..." He closed his lips.

"I like it here," Brad said.

"Do you have to contradict everything I say?"

"I was just saying I like it here."

"I heard you the first time." Brad's dad locked the door and banged it. "You're at least a foot from the curb, Una."

The Traynors, all four of them, came surging across the lawn. Introductions were made all round.

"Why don't you kids watch a video, while we grownups chat?" Mrs. Traynor took the pecan pie and led the way into the house. It smelled of spaghetti sauce and garlic bread.

"Lasagna?" Brad asked, rubbing his stomach in anticipation.

"It's your favorite," Kenny grinned. "What about snack food, Dad?"

Grant Traynor handed over a tray of nachos and soft drinks. He was wearing his favorite white and blue Icelandic sweater and ironed jeans. Mrs. Traynor had on a blue silk jump suit. They looked comfortable together, and looking at them, relaxed and casual like that, Brad could see how much younger than his mom and dad they were.

"What a lovely house." Brad's dad's voice deepened. "You must be an interior decorator as well as a great cook, Mrs. Traynor." He stood in the vestibule, tall, handsome, distinguished-looking with those striking eyes and narrow face. He smiled broadly.

"Call me Anna."

"What perfume is that?" Desmond took Anna Traynor's hand.

"Let's get out of here, Brad," Lane whispered. "Before I bring up."

"Is your dad always so charming?" Kenny drawled 'charming' like he had a Southern accent. "He doesn't look like he's been sick in the head. What's it like having a dad who's been in a mental hospital?"

"Shut up, Kenny," Lane said. The three of them operated seriously on the nachos. Brad loaded the video and threw himself down on the old plaid couch in the Traynor family room. He gulped cola. Darkness like ocean depths washed through his head. His ears drummed like he was coming up in a bathysphere and needed decompression.

"I can't do anything right according to him."

"Your dad's nervous, coming back after a year, trying to fit in," Lane said. She paused the video. "You've moved, your mother's got a good job, you've grown six inches and then some." Lane poured more salsa on the last few nachos. "Most personal problems come down to issues of control, power or money. That's what Aunt Peebles talked about in Socials last week, remember? Human beings don't like change. Your family is going through a big change right now."

"Does he have to be so grouchy?"

"We've got one grouchy Grandma," Kenny laughed. "We don't visit her often."

"I've got to live with him every day, Kenny."

"He dresses great. His hair is long. He plays a great piano. What more do you want?"

I don't know, Brad said to himself. *Something different than I've got.*

"Shut up, Kenny." Lane turned to look at Brad more closely.

"What about family counseling?" she asked. "You've a lot more years of this."

Brad frowned. "If they won't talk to me about anything, they sure aren't going to talk to any family counsellor." His voice had raised to a shout, partly so he could be heard over the TV and partly because he was talking about something so personal that he wanted it to go away. He wished Lane would stop making him think about this stuff. "Besides, I think he already sees a therapist. So he won't have another breakdown or whatever." Brad blushed.

"Have you really tried talking to him?" Lane asked.

"Talk to him? Are you kidding? He puts me down all the time? Makes me feel like a dolt," Brad shouted.

"Hey, you're the greatest, snackface." Kenny banged him on the back so hard a chip lodged in Brad's throat. He coughed and spluttered.

Grant Traynor hollered from the other room. "Are you guys okay?"

"Sure, Dad, we're fine." Kenny turned "Star Trek" back on. Brad slouched in the corner of the couch.

"Trust my nosey sister, Miss Let's-fix-it of the '90s." Kenny passed Brad the chips. "She doesn't know when to leave people alone."

"Watch the show, Kenny," Lane hissed.

★

Later after supper the Traynors and the Greaves gathered in the living room. Grant got out his guitar. Kenny plugged in his acoustic keyboard. Desmond sat at the piano. Una, Anna and the kids sang.

"You have an exceptional alto voice, my dear," Brad's dad smiled up into Anna's face. "I used to train choirs, but it became too much for me." Anna Traynor's face flushed with pleasure.

"I sing in the church choir," she said.

"You have a great sense of rhythm, boy." Desmond tousled Kenny's hair. "I was born with rhythm in my bones. I won every prize in my category at the provincial music festival when I was your age."

Brad's dad passed out compliments like chocolates to all the Traynors. They stopped singing when their throats got dry. Cocoa and biscuits finished the evening.

"What a charming man your husband is," Anna Traynor said to Brad's mom as she helped Una on with her coat. "You must be glad to have him home."

"We are, aren't we, Brad?"

Brad knelt tying his sneakers. His fingers fumbled with the laces. He said nothing.

"You seem awfully quiet, Brad," Grant Traynor said at the door.

"Thanks for the lovely dinner." Brad's voice sounded tired.

"Goodnight all. Goodnight." Then Grant added, "Don't forget the Scout camping weekend is coming soon. Can you get someone to cover your route for you? We really want you to come."

Brad nodded. The door closed.

"What a noisy family." Desmond slid into the front passenger seat. "Three hours with them and I'm exhausted."

☆

Brad stood on the corner close to Buckles' house. Two big black motorcycles were parked on the lawn, if you could call the weed-strewn plot of ground a lawn.

Brad shivered. He zippered his jacket and gulped as if he were an astronaut on Mars. He had to talk to Buckles. Brad couldn't think of anyone else who would deliver the papers if he went on the Scout camping weekend. Besides, Buckles knew the route. Communicating with Mission Control from Mars would be easier, even with the four-minute delay between each wave of radio communications. Earth would be the brightest star in the Martian sky. A big improvement over the squashed beer cans and dirt by Buckles' house.

Raucous laughter and the noise of a blaring TV came from the gray stucco one-and-a-half-storey house with a Canadian flag covering the basement window. Aluminum foil filled the attic window.

Brad squared his shoulders. Before he lost his nerve he hurried up the steps and hammered on the partly-open door. The door swung open, revealing burly people on couches and chairs, beer bottles and cigarettes on coffee tables. The place smelled of sweat and cooking oil.

"Whatdyawan, kid?" one guy asked.

"Yousesellinsumpin?" a skinny black man in torn jeans and an L.A Kings t-shirt mumbled from the hallway. Buckles erupted from the kitchen. His eyes were wild. He pushed Brad out the door and down the rickety steps.

"Introduce us to your friend, Rory," the first guy hollered.

"What do ya want, wimp bucket?" Buckles urged Brad towards the curb. "What do ya want? I haven't messed with your precious papers or nuthin', don't mess with me—or ya'll be sorry."

Brad blinked several times. The red in his face spread to the roots of his hair.

"If you wanna talk to me, bozo, do it at school," Buckles strode towards the back lane.

"You haven't been there for two days," Brad shouted back. "I need you to do my papers this weekend. The Scouts are going camping."

"Do your papers, do your papers." Buckles squatted against the partly painted fence. The unpainted slats grayed in the wind like uneven teeth.

"I'll pay you double for Saturday and Sunday." Brad squatted beside him. His knees cracked.

Buckles lit a cigarette butt. "Cash. Only do it for cash." He took a deep drag. "Now. Right now."

"How do I know you'll do them?" Brad coughed, stood up.

"Smoke bother ya? I bet ya haven't even tried one, have ya. Such a goody-goody. I hate goody-goody guys." He mumbled on. "Camping, camping, well la-dee-da."

Brad took out his wallet, handed two ten dollar bills to Buckles with the list of house numbers for his route. "Old Mr. Drum likes his paper early. Mrs. Chan wants it stuck between the screen and the front door."

"Let 'em suffer for a couple of days." Buckles shoved the money in his pocket, knocked the ash off his butt and put it in a crushed packet, hunched his shoulders and turned away.

"Do you collect hockey cards?" Brad didn't want the other boy to leave. "I've got an original Wayne Gretzky."

"Big deal."

Inside the house someone screamed, bodies crashed against furniture. Glass shattered. A man howled, then all went silent.

Buckles shrugged, shoved his hands deep into his pockets. "What are ya standing there for? Bug off." Buckles crept up the back steps and peered in.

"Don't ever come around here again, ya hear. I told you, I don't need goody-goody guys hangin' around."

Brad's sneakers crunched on gravel as he walked. He turned several times to study the back of Buckles' house. He paused, clenched and unclenched his fists, rubbed the back of his neck, exhaled three times. Buckles lived on a different planet, one with a hostile environment, one where life would be difficult, hard to sustain. Not like Traynors', certainly not like Brad's place.

"I'll get you one of these days, Bradley," a voice taunted from an upstairs window. "I haven't forgotten ya knocked me down, bozo. Nobody, but nobody pushes me around and gets away with it, yahearme."

Brad raced away.

"Nobody." The voice followed him.

At home he tiptoed past the philodendron. Some student was playing Schubert. "Nice, very nice, Mrs. Timms, but please try to pay more attention to the rhythm."

"You play so well," Mrs. Timms said.

"I won top prize in the Conservatory. I could have been a concert pianist but ..." Bradley gritted his teeth, forgot the tiptoeing and pounded up the stairs to his room. He had no patience with showoffs or bullies, he didn't care what had made them that way. A person has to make his own decisions.

"Bradley, is that you, dear?" his mother called.

"Yes, Mom." It would be so great to get out of the house for the weekend. He needed a break.

His backpack leaned by the wall. Brad checked the top pocket for the compass and knife. All he was missing were the binoculars. They were outside fastened to the camera tripod by the equatorial mounting he had made from plans he'd gotten at the planetarium. All he had to do was point the axis at the Pole Star, and the binoculars would track the stars as they moved across the sky. He'd covered the whole outfit with waterproof plastic and chained it to the balcony.

Brad swung one leg over the balcony railing and scooted down the folding ladder he'd built. He unlocked the back shed where all his tools were now neatly arranged. The photo of Grandpa Greaves hung on the wall beside the set square. He was standing beside a real big guy, a tough-looking dude.

Boy, that Rory Buckholz was tough. Small, but tough. Brad felt mad and sad at the same time. It was confusing. People were hard to understand.

Brad grabbed the tools he needed for the camping trip and was about to lock the door when the buzzer he'd rigged up from the kitchen went off. That would be mom. He buzzed her back and locked the shed door, loped across the laneway, tripping over a bag of fertilizer that smelled like cow dung.

"Your father and I were wondering whether you should be neglecting your chores this weekend." His mother was using her adult real eastate lady voice. Una May Greaves was making tea and cinnamon toast for her husband. "Besides, Desmond has an audition in the city tomorrow and the house will be empty."

Brad leaned against the back door clutching his tool belt

for the trip, blinking.

"Like a cup of tea?"

Think. Think fast, Brad.

His father was ushering Mrs. Timms out the front door.

"You're making real progress," he said. His voice was deep and gentle. "Don't forget to practice now."

Brad looked at his mother. Suggesting Brad stay home was not her idea. He and his mom had never stewed about being away a day or two. Like Kenny, his dad was like Kenny, only more so, a real worrywart.

"Rory Buckholz is doing my papers, Mom. I mowed the lawn yesterday, and I'll clean the upstairs bathroom before I go to bed." He joined her at the stove. "Old Drum can keep an eye on the place so you can go with Dad and have a good time together." He carried the full teapot with the thin wisps of vapor circling around it like a small atmospheric cloud around a planetoid. The tea smelled of tannin and lemon.

"Old Drum can keep an eye on the place," his mother repeated what Brad had said, the kicked-in side of her face struggling with a smile. "Like he used to when you and I went on a jaunt to the city."

Brad took a swallow of hot tea and reached for a piece of cinnamon toast. The air in the kitchen was warmer than it had been in weeks.

"We don't get much time to talk, you and I." Una May sat down beside Brad. "Not since Desmond came home. You seem so busy these days, with Scouts and school and all your projects."

Brad nodded.

"You'd tell me if you were unhappy, wouldn't you?"

She pulled her chair closer to the table. Brad could smell her flowery perfume. "You're so grown up, so big for your

★ 48 ★

age, a young man, a serious young man. I don't know where the time has gone."

Brad still didn't say anything.

"I guess teenagers have a hard time talking to their parents."

"I'm all right, Mom," Brad said, stiffly.

"Your father can be difficult, I know." She reached out as if to pat Brad's knee but pulled back and rubbed her palm down her own dark blue skirt in a nervous series of strokes. "Desmond is set in his ways. Always has been. That's one reason I had you. I thought being a mother would make my life better." She pressed her lips together. "It did for a while, didn't it?"

She continued. "I shouldn't complain, I've been very fortunate in many ways. I wanted a family and I've got one, for now anyway." His mother wasn't talking to him anymore; she was talking to herself.

Once when he was in first or second grade, Brad had eaten all the chocolate chip cookies, and then found out his mom had made them for his school lunches. Her voice sounded the same now. Was he to blame for some sadness she carried with her? By growing up was he stealing her happiness? He pushed away from the table as if it were an enemy.

The front door banged. His father came down the hall. "That woman has no sense of rhythm and she is grossly overweight. I can't stand undisciplined people. Una May, whatever you do, don't get fat on me."

Brad drained his cup and ran it under the tap and grabbed one last slice of toast.

He would have to trust his mother to engineer his safe escape to the woods. The Scouts were going camping at Blueberry Creek. They were supposed to build a bridge at Peebles' summer place, have campfires and wiener roasts. It would be good training. Only last week Brad had read that most people chosen to be astronauts had been in Scouts or air cadets. The next step would be some real wilderness training, like Outward Bound or a Voyager trip down one of Canada's big rivers. He had his escape route mapped out. It was surviving the day-to-day now that worried him, finding space for himself. Would the night sky be enough?

Out on the balcony he aimed the binoculars toward the evening star, Venus—beautiful to look at but deadly to live on—its atmosphere mostly carbon monoxide, the temperature 900 degrees Fahrenheit and the clouds full of sulphur and hydrochloric acid droplets. Inhospitable. Unfriendly, like Buckles' place.

Mars, the red planet, windswept and dusty. Now, Mars was friendlier. In a space suit Brad could stand on Mars and look back at the Earth and with a good telescope see Earth's oceans and land masses. What a view that would be. A warm, rich, bright feeling blazed inside Brad, moving faster than blood or plasma, filling his chest and diaphragm with sensations similar to roller-coaster rides, fast elevators, or landing planes. Brad didn't know what to call this physical sense of wonder, this sense of standing outside oneself, outside time or space in the light. He couldn't be the only one who felt it. It must be a human thing. No words could describe it. He didn't try, he let it wash over him like lake water on a hot summer day.

Brad unlocked his binoculars, removed them from the tripod and carried them inside. He put them in their case and set the case beside the backpack and tool belt.

He wasn't going to be able to sleep, he was too excited. He lay in bed with his hands behind his head, his elbows splayed on the pillow, staring through the window at the familiar pattern of the planets and stars, the predictable, astonishing arc of flickering lights. The night sky glowed above Camden. A few streetlights, floodlights, neon signposts hinted of a town on the edge of a dark expanse of prairie. Camden was like a small planet on the edge of a sea of grass. The solar system was perched on the edge of a middle-aged galaxy in an expanding universe. Wonder reached inside Brad and stretched him beyond his limits, beyond the fights and squabbles. He pulled the light wool blanket to his chin. His thoughts made him dizzy, so he turned his mind to practical problems.

If they sunk the wooden poles a foot and a half into the ground would that make the bridge strong enough? Should they lash the crosspieces or nail them? Depended if they went by the book or made modifications. There was something secure about following the rules, but then, sometimes Brad knew he had to adapt and change to suit the situation. The important thing was to get it right.

5. THE CAMPING TRIP

Oh you can't get to heaven
in a motor boat
'cause there's no river
where you can float.

KENNY AND AZIM Kanji, Camden's newest and skinniest Scout, shouted out the window of the old Honda as it barreled down the side road towards Peebles' farm. Brad stared at the passing fields, feeling uncomfortable. That song or the buffeting car brought on waves of nausea, knotting his throat so he couldn't sing.

A memory flooded back; his dad's students singing that song in the dark house long ago. A group of big boys gathered around his father, laughing and singing. In the kitchen there had been a tub of fancy ice cream, balloons, and a cake to celebrate something. Brad had been sent to bed early. His mother had smuggled both of them a bowl of neapolitan ice cream with candy sprinkles on top. They had sat side by side on Brad's bed savoring every bite of the wonderful sweet mixture, while the music and excited voices of his dad and those piano students continued downstairs. Had he been old enough to notice that his mother's face looked nearly as sad as his own, or was he just realizing it now?

The cords in Brad's neck were tight as fence wire. His knees were jammed against the seat in front of him.

He turned his attention to the fields, tried to estimate the size by counting the number of fenceposts and the distance between them. Mr. Traynor concentrated on driving. Mrs. Traynor, with Lane and Ashley, bumped along behind them in the van. Mr. Bates, Bruce's dad, followed slowly, driving his station wagon. Bruce, called Bait because he liked fishing so much, sleepy Terry Junk, and tiny Tommy Ho were riding in the wagon.

"Did you ever see a goat in a motor boat …" Kenny sounded hoarse. "Why aren't you singing, Brad?"

Brad chewed a fingernail and avoided Kenny's eyes.

As the car accelerated around the next curve, a tractor loomed, hauling a double wide rake, moving slowly toward them. Grant frantically swerved, pumped the brakes and headed for the ditch on the other side of the road. He barely missed the tractor. The Honda bounced and bumped down the shoulder.

"Dad, Dad, the brakes!" Kenny screamed.

Brad banged his knees so badly his upper legs ached.

"No problem," Mr. Traynor sighed as the Honda came to rest beside an immense anthill. "Takes a little pumping that's all." He sat clutching the steering wheel, shaking his head. "I replaced the brake shoes last week. It must be something else."

The van had stopped. The road was covered with people scurrying like ants spilled out of their hill.

"Are you guys okay?" Lane and Ashley leaned into the back seat. Ashley's long blond hair blew across Brad's face. She smelled like lilacs. Brad blushed.

Azim Kanji, skinny as a stick, stood by the side of the road in a daze. His dark skin shone with sweat, his black hair fell over his broad forehead. His dark brown eyes were startled as a deer's, his angular frame quivered as he half laughed, half cried. "My uncle Mohammed drives like that." His face relaxed into a grin, "No wonder my mother won't ride with him."

"Dad, you need to get the car fixed by a real mechanic." Kenny frowned so deeply the kids could have planted watermelon seeds in the ridges on his forehead. "You keep promising."

Mr. Traynor dusted off the knees of his jeans. "I know, I know. I think the clutch is going. The brakes are fine if you pump them."

"You are so stubborn, Grant," his wife Anna chided.

The farmer on his giant John Deere tractor was staring back at them shaking his head. Grant started towards him, looking sheepish. "I better apologize."

"Besides, Dad, we look dumb," Lane protested.

Mr. Bates pulled alongside. "Trouble?"

"Mr. Traynor got squeezed off the road by that tractor," Ashley said. "It was pretty funny watching them riding on the shoulder. I thought they'd never stop. Better than a car chase on TV." She giggled.

Brad squinted in the sunlight. How could a girl look so great and sound so silly? They'd nearly had an accident and Ashley Sargent thought it was funny. His impatience with people grew by the minute. First Mr. Traynor has a dumb accident and now Ashley talks dumb. Why couldn't they be sensible?

Mr. Bates started his car and headed towards Peebles' driveway a half a kilometer ahead. Matt Peebles stood in the middle of the dusty road, waving them on like a traffic cop.

Mrs. Traynor and the girls climbed back into the van and drove off, too. Brad and Azim folded their legs into the back seat. Kenny rode up front with his Dad. "We could have been hurt, Dad. You drive too fast. The car needs repairs."

"You worry too much, Kenny." His father punched Kenny's arm and started up the Honda's engine. Billows of exhaust fogged the road. "This car is a precious antique," Kenny's father continued. "We bought it when you were born."

Kenny was silent, glaring through the windscreen, drumming his fingers on his knee as if he was practicing scales on a piano with sticky keys. His lips were pressed tightly together. "Sometimes I think I was adopted. What's a nice worrywart, neatfreak like me doing in a family of warm fuzzy do-it-tomorrow type people." His words were jokey but he sounded serious.

Azim and Brad glanced at each other and shrugged. It wasn't great being caught in the middle of other people's family fights.

The car moved slowly down the road to the farm. A vein in Brad's neck pulsed. It was so good to get away from home, away from the plants and the piano and his folks. He took a deep breath.

"I will not tell my mother," Azim whispered. "About the little accident. She worries all the time. Life is so different in India."

"Mine won't worry." Brad said. "They've got enough worries of their own." He sighed and leaned his head against the seat.

He should forget about people for awhile, concentrate on books and TV. He'd just watched a great series of TV programs on PBS about astronomers. They work at night and sleep during the day. Giant telescopes in Mexico, South America, Hawaii, and California scanned the sky. If he decided to do that he'd have to go to school for years and years and read libraries full of books. And leave home. That would be all right.

He'd be an astronaut but they have to get along with other people, be physically fit, and able to stand weightlessness. He was good at the books and loved the sky and the thought of getting close to the planets, but people made him uncomfortable. He never knew what to say.

"It's about time you guys got here." Bait, Junk and Tommy Ho jumped from the log gate at the entrance to the farm. "The Peebles have orange juice and doughnuts." The three boys led the way.

"That's probably the last real food we'll get," Tommy Ho snickered.

"I could catch some fish." Bait giggled.

"We've got a bridge to build," Kenny scolded. "I want to win the prize not major in eating."

Junk moaned.

"We won't have curry, thank goodness. I'm sick of curry," Azim said. "I want hot dogs."

"If Matt Peebles leaves any for us," laughed Kenny. "He eats everything in sight."

Brad strolled along with his hands in his pockets. Tommy Ho had to walk fast to keep up. Junk had a long stride but he looked half-asleep most of the time. He was even quieter than Brad. Around the bend in the lane they came upon the house.

Brad whistled between his teeth. Peebles' summer cabin was really a gorgeous log home of imported cedar with sky lights and a chalet roof, long windows, porches, balconies and decks running in every direction. Birds fluttered around the overhanging eaves, a raven screamed from the woods by the creek.

Dr. Peebles handed out glasses of juice. Mrs. Peebles passed a big box of doughnuts, every variety under the sun. Brad grabbed a chocolate one with coconut icing and stuffed it in his mouth, turning back to study the house. "This is just for summer?"

"And weekends when Dr. Peebles isn't on call," Mrs. Peebles grinned and held the box under Brad's nose. He took another doughnut. "We wanted a place where the whole family, Traynors and Peebles, could get away. Teachers like Grant and I need time off for good behavior, Brad."

Grant and Mrs. Peebles were sister and brother. They both taught in the same school and had kids the same age. Probably when Kenny and Lane grew up they'd follow the same pattern, stay in Camden and work, marry and have kids. Not him, though. He'd move. Something would happen, it always did. Only this time Brad would be old enough to figure things out. He wasn't a little kid any more.

"Let's find a place to camp, Brad." Kenny yanked his arm. Brad followed, wiping sticky hands on back pockets, feeling the scratch of the rivets snag at his palms, making them tingle, not hurt like they had when he'd grabbed Buckles by the collar.

"Did I tell you about Buckles' house?" He caught up with Kenny and the two of them sauntered along while he told Kenny about his visit. "It smelled bad."

"Watch out for that dude," Kenny climbed over a broken-down fence. "He's mean."

"Living around punks like those guys, no wonder." Brad stood eyeing a sunlit valley with a big willow and a tall pine. Masses of pine needles coated the ground.

"There's a great place to camp." Kenny pointed. "The pine needles will make our beds soft. I hate sleeping on bare ground." Kenny ran down the hill, bent and tossed handfuls of needles in the air. "Come on, slowpoke, brainface, knobnose."

Hands in his pockets Brad walked down the hill. "Let's check it out carefully. We don't want to be too far away from water, or too close to animal dens."

"Look who's the worrywart now." Kenny twirled around once. "The sooner we set up camp, the sooner we can start on the bridge."

"What drives your engine, Kenny?" Brad asked.

"What do you mean? I like doing stuff, that's all. Sitting around is boring," Kenny answered, sounding a little miffed. He ran up the slope towards the house and back down just for the heck of it.

Kenny and Lane were so different. Lane wanted to talk about people and how Brad was doing. Kenny just wanted to joke, work or play. Lane gave him a funny feeling and he didn't know whether it was her being a good-looking girl or her being interested in how he felt about things. Some things he wasn't ready for yet.

Brad toured the space around their chosen camping spot before he followed Kenny. It was protected from the wind, had plenty of flat ground for Kenny's pup tent. A twinge of doubt crossed Brad's mind as he stepped in some muddy grass flats behind their camp site. If there was a bad storm would this gooey area grow?

At the top of the hill perched on a rock Kenny sat sharpening his knife on a stone, whistling Bach or Beethoven.

"I'm worried about the mud."

"The pine needles are great." Kenny said. He had collected quite a pile for his bed and was hoping to sleep comfortably.

"If it rains ..."

"Get your stuff, Brad, for crying out loud." Kenny tossed

a handful of dead grass at him. Brad scurried to bring his sleeping bag and mess kit. He checked the hooks on his belt, where his Swiss army knife and leather-holstered hunting knife hung. He was proud of those. He'd bought them with paper route cash. Brad liked buying things he needed, it made him feel independent.

He enjoyed books about kids being independent. He'd read one about an English kid who had run away from home when he was twelve and bicycled across Europe. He'd been abused. Brad didn't need to run away, but he needed to escape every once in a while when life got too dark or complicated. He wouldn't mind camping out here all alone, with his binoculars, a pile of books and a few tools.

The 1st Camden Scout troop, close buddies and good friends, pitched their tents. Ashley and Lane set up camp close to the house. Azim and Matt disappeared behind a clump of aspen. Sleepy Terry Junk, Bait and tiny Tommy Ho were already hammering pegs near the corner of the field closest to the creek.

"If the creek floods you'll get wet," Brad shouted.

6. WASHOUT

MR. BATES CALLED the troop for dinner. He had laid out salads and buns and soft drinks on a long folding table on the bank of the stream. A freshly-painted picnic table loaded down with two gas stoves, cooking pots and supplies sat nearby. Benches circled the campfire. Brad threw his sweater on a bench near the fire and headed for the food. He was famished. It didn't seem to matter how often he ate these days, he was hungry most of the time.

"I'm glad we didn't have to bring our own food." Tommy Ho shoved three hot dogs onto one forked stick. The rich smells of cooking meat filled the air.

"We're concentrating on the bridge project this weekend," Grant said. "With two other troops competing, we'll have our hands full building the bridge."

"Bet the 2nd Scout Troop are doing a baby project," Kenny sneered. Ever since the near-accident on the road in to Peebles', Kenny's voice had sounded sharp as a steak knife when he talked to his dad.

"Trevor asked the Warden for a project," Mrs. Traynor said. She was director of Public Relations for the regional Parks Department. "I helped choose a good one. Kenny, what's your problem?"

"The 2nd Scouts are a couple of miles away at the provincial park," Grant added. "Building a walking trail from the creek to the river."

"That's not like building a bridge." Kenny punched the bottom of the ketchup bottle. It spurted all over his hamburger and his t-shirt. He wiped the spill with his hand, spreading it all over, then he inhaled the hamburger and grabbed a smokie.

"What about the Venturers?" Lane gave her brother a pitying look. "What are they doing?"

"Building a new outhouse in the park," Mr. Bates said. "My brother's kids are with them. Plenty of digging."

"Pee-yew! Who wants to build a biffy?" Ashley quipped. "This whole trip seems pretty silly and babyish if you ask me. I might ruin my hair and I'll smell like smoke for a week."

"The biffy doesn't smell until later, dummy, and a little smoke won't hurt you." Lane leaned so close to the fire Brad could smell her eyelashes singeing. He pushed her back from the flames. "Oh, Bradley, you saved my life." She giggled. She and Ashley cast their eyes skyward.

"You're too serious, Bradley," Ashley said.

"Much too serious," Lane added. "And Kenny's so mad at dad he's pouring ketchup on himself."

"Lay off, will you." Kenny waved his cooking stick at the two girls. His smokie dropped in the dirt. "Shoot, it was just cooked, too."

"So dust it off." Brad picked it up, wiped it on his jeans and handed it to Kenny. Kenny put it on the picnic table and got a new one. Brad shook his head.

For a few minutes the quietness and munching and the sounds and smells of low flames cooking hot dogs pulled the troop together in a cluster. Like stars in the Milky Way, thought Brad. He was not alone. He was part of something bigger than himself, his family and the darkness that threatened.

"Camp inspection in thirty minutes, troop," Mr. Traynor said. "Campfire in one hour. Lights out at 9:30." The kids groaned. "We want to get an early start tomorrow."

Kenny and Brad hurried away with smokies in hand. They had to finish setting up. The sound of classical music floated down the hill from Peebles' place. The two boys worked quickly and quietly, tidying their sleeping bags, knapsacks, sweeping out the tent, listening to the music.

"It's Holst, the *Planets*," Brad said. "Jupiter, bringer of greatness and joy. I could stand some."

"Tell me about it." Kenny was shoving a pile of pine needles under his side of the tent to make it softer. "I get so cheesed off with my dad sometimes."

"Me, too." Brad fastened the clips on his knapsack.

"My dad can't play piano," Kenny said. "I've heard your dad play. He's really good. He liked the way I played. Did you hear what he said about me? Too bad he doesn't teach kids. He's better than my teacher."

"Look, you like him so much, you live with him, okay. You tiptoe around the place while the maestro performs. Our house is too small by half. You don't have to share your life with a piano."

"Are you jealous of your dad's piano, fuzzbrain?"

Blood pounded in Brad's temples. Maybe if he didn't say anything Kenny would shut up. Can you tell your best friend to mind his own business?

"Aren't you glad he came home?" Kenny asked. "My dad never goes away. He's such a mess. Never puts his tools away. Drives mom nuts 'cause he promises to fix things. Your dad is more organized and he's talented besides."

"Just forget it, okay. Lay off!" Brad took his knife off his belt and pried open the small blade, started scoring the bark of the pine tree, running his knife down its side, pushing hard against the black sap, smelling the piney scent. Pine trees live for hundreds of years if they aren't scarred or infected with bugs. Brad pried two grubs from the bark and flung them into the deep bush.

"What a quiet campsite," Mr. Traynor came lumbering down the hill with Mr. Bates. "Problems, boys?"

Kenny and Brad shook their heads, avoided each others' eyes and stood erect, watching as Grant and Mr. Bates inspected.

"Who's the one with the thick mattress of pine needles?" Mr. Bates chuckled. "What ever happened to roughing it in the woods?"

Grant peered at their choice of location. "A little mushy back there." He pointed to the grassy strip behind the pine tree.

"It's protected from the wind," Brad said.

"It's not the wind that's got me worried." Grant scratched his head and moved off.

Brad closed his knife and hung it back on his belt, strolled to the grassy strip and studied the mud flats. Then he headed into the darkening woods, picking his way through the rose and gooseberry bushes until he found a deer track. He ran, ducking branches and leaping deadfall. He could hear his heart beating and feel his breath going in and out, in and out. He was very much alive. If only Kenny hadn't talked to him like that. It made him feel stupid and angry and he didn't like it.

"Brad, hey, Brad, where are you?" Kenny's voice followed him. Brad headed towards the creek, tripped on a root and sprawled face down on the forest floor, winding himself.

He propped up at the base of a tree and caught his breath, sat with hands wrapped around his knees listening to the darkness and savoring the musky odours of decaying plants and trees. Coyotes, a chattering ground squirrel and a hermit thrush sang bedtime songs. He checked his watch. Time to get back.

Brad opened his compass and turned towards the campsite, pushing and shoving his way through prickles and boughs until he came out where the kids were gathered around the roaring fire.

"Fire's burning, fire's burning, draw nearer, draw nearer," the troop sang.

Brad sat on a log between Tommy Ho and Azim. Neither one of them were close buddies. They'd leave him alone.

☆

An hour later Kenny and Brad, with the help of flashlights, found their way back to their tent. Brad hadn't said a word all evening.

"So, why don't you just tell me to shut up?" Kenny pushed Brad down on the ground in front of their tent and sat on his chest. Brad rolled Kenny over and pinned him down. Sweat ran into his eyes. Kenny's hair picked up strands of dead grass and pine needles. The two of them struggled and rolled until Brad was sitting on Kenny's chest again.

"So, shut up, Kenny." Brad let go and rolled off. The two of them crawled into their sleeping bags. "Mind your own business."

"Lane said you were mad." Kenny burrowed deep into his pine needles. "She said you and your dad don't get along and I shouldn't bug you about it. Did I bug you?"

Brad threw a dirty gym sock onto Kenny's face. Laughter echoed from some other campsite.

"Sphinx," Kenny said.

"Sphinx?"

"Sitting saying nothing for years on end." Kenny rolled over. The pine needles crackled beneath him. Coyotes howled. A bull bellowed. Another bull farther away hollered back.

"So much for the silent woods," Brad said.

The tent fluttered in the wind.

"Are you asleep?" Kenny asked.

"Nope," Brad chewed his lip. "I've been trying to figure out how to fill out my family tree for Mrs. Peebles."

"Haven't you handed that in yet?" Kenny raised up on his left elbow. "Lane and I did ours together. It took two sheets what with cousins and second cousins once removed." He giggled.

"I wish I could borrow a few," Brad sighed. "Mine are all dead or miles away. My folks won't talk. Say it's none of my business."

"Weird, man," Kenny spoke low like a macho boxer. "Aren't you their kid?"

"So, what do I do?"

"You're as bad as I am," Kenny laughed. "Handing in assignments, finishing projects, we gotta do it."

"Maybe I could say I lost it."

"Brad, you've never lost homework yet," Kenny snorted. "No, it's gotta be better than that. I wonder what Lane would say?"

"She'd probably invent a whole family for me."

A cricket chirped by the tent flap, a stray moth banged against the tent wall.

"That's it, bozobreath. We'll invent a scad of absent relatives, or make Old Drum your grandpa. Wait till we tell

Lane, she'll love it."

"What if someone discovers it's fake?" Brad asked.

"So, we'll tell the truth. Your folks are hiding something."

Brad's shoulders tightened, his mouth went dry. "Shut up, Kenny."

"Right," the voice across the tent mumbled. "It's none of my business."

"Not knowing stuff makes me nervous," Brad whispered.

"Did you say something?" Kenny asked.

"Go to sleep, Kenny."

"Go to sleep, Brad."

☆

Brad woke with a start. Rain pounded on the tent roof like hailstones on a trampoline. Maybe it *was* hailstones. Kenny was snuffling like a pig in mud. Water poured through the tent flap.

"Buffalo biscuits! Brad, wake up, we're drowning," Kenny's voice was squeaky and shrill. Suddenly the tent caved in and dropped on the two boys hunkered on the soggy floor.

Wind tore at the flaps. Trees snapped and whistled in the gale.

"Brad, Kenny, are you all right?" Mr. Traynor's voice called over the whine of the wind.

The boys fought with the cloaking nylon and pushed their way out into the black night. The sharp smell of rain-soaked earth and wet grass filled the air. Brad shivered, the cold water splashed his skin. A torrent of water surged around them.

"Some safe spot, Bradley," Kenny said as he lunged up the hill towards his father.

"We chose it together," Brad reminded him.

Dr. Peebles' four-by-four sat at the top of the slope. The headlights shone on the washout. He rolled the window down. "Climb in."

Brad and Kenny jumped into the little red truck and it wheeled and spun up the hill to the house.

"What about the rest of the kids?" Kenny asked.

"They are fine," laughed Grant. "They picked drier spots."

Brad scrunched his face. Kenny and he stared at each other. They looked like drowned rats, hair plastered to their heads, pajamas plastered to their bodies.

Brad didn't know whether to laugh or cry.

"I thought you two might learn a lesson." Grant led them to a back bedroom where they towelled off and settled for the rest of the night.

"The kids are going to give us a hard time." Kenny pulled one of Dr. Peebles' t-shirts over his head. It came to his knees.

"We think we're smart," Brad was combing his hair. It stuck out all over if he didn't. He didn't need the kids laughing about that as well.

"We are most of the time," Kenny sighed.

"Not this time." Brad flipped off the light switch.

"We would have been all right if it hadn't rained." Kenny blew his nose.

"Yeah, but it rained, didn't it?" Brad shook his head on the pillow. He should have figured out about that grassy river flowing behind the willow and made Kenny move. A good Scout is responsible. "Forget it, okay," Kenny yawned. "Let's go to sleep."

7. BUILDING BRIDGES

ONLY THE BIRDS and Venus watched as Brad moved the soggy tent from where they had left it after its collapse and their dousing. The sun came over the cliff and Venus disappeared.

Brad pegged the tent securely on the edge of the open field near the slope to their former campsite. He had a plan. First he strung a clothesline from a pine tree to a spindly birch and hung out Kenny's and his bedding. Next he found another pair of trees down in the valley where the grassy river had receded, leaving no evidence of the deluge. He strung a second clothesline out of sight. Brad hung up their sodden pajamas and backpacks. The sun didn't reach this spot, but at least the other kids wouldn't see them. That was important. His feet flew over the grass, running up the hill to the log cabin.

"Wake up, Kenny." Brad nudged the curled-up form. "Come help."

"Whaaat?" Kenny moaned. "It isn't even morning yet. Go back to bed, Bradwurst. I hate morning people."

Brad tugged at Kenny's right hand hanging loose, fingers touching the floor. "Do you want the kids to laugh at us bunking in here like a couple of preschoolers?"

"In where?" Kenny rubbed his eyes and stuck his feet on

the floor. "Oh, shoot. This isn't the tent." He peeked brown eyes through the tanned hands covering his face. "Can we fool them?"

Brad tiptoed along the hall and dashed down the hill. Kenny, pulling on damp shorts from the bottom of his pile of wet clothes, ran to catch up. "Wait for me."

Brad placed a stump in front of the tent. He sat down and began whittling a birch stick with his knife. "Try to look nonchalant, Kenny, like we've been here for ages."

"We could tell them we moved. They don't have to know why—unless dad or Dr. Peebles squeal on us." Kenny ran his fingers through his hair. "I hate feeling dumb." Kenny whistled a cheery tune and straightened a tent peg.

Brad nodded. He was just pointing out where the hidden clothesline was when Azim and Matt came striding over the hill. Both Brad and Kenny tried to look relaxed and casual. A group of chickadees squabbled in a nearby pine. An early rising fly pestered Brad's thumb, attracted to the glint of his knife as it rhythmically peeled bark from the chunk of birch.

"Boy, I thought this was a war zone last night," Azim laughed. "My uncle Mohammed has floodlights on his front lawn that aren't as bright as Dr. Peebles' four-by-four when they rescued our brainy friends from their watery trough."

"Smart move, fellows." Matt was eating a cinnamon bun, and butter clung to his chin.

Kenny shrugged and glanced over at Brad. He was furiously paring the birch. A pile of shavings grew by his feet.

"Well, if it isn't the last of Noah's survivors—you remember the animals went in two by two—you guys ended up going in a four-by-four. Ha!" Ashley and Lane giggled as they hurried past to the fire pit. Lane pushed around the wet coals looking for an ember.

Tommy Ho and Bait joined the crowd moving towards the ash-filled fire pit. "What's up?" Tommy asked.

"Brad and Kenny camped in a river," Ashley said.

"The brains bombed out," Matt joked.

"Pretty dumb place to camp," Bait chuckled. "We slept through. Junk is still sleeping."

"I thought Brad knew better," Azim said.

"The way Kenny worries about everything." Tommy Ho slapped his leg.

"Enough. Get the fire started," Mr. Bates frowned. "Breakfast." He laid out the food. "Cereal, juice and milk. You lazybones can cook your own toast. Keep your minds off bickering." He tousled his son's hair.

"Did you hear about Brad and Kenny?" Bait asked his dad. "What a dumb move they made."

"Lay off, for Pete's sake!" Brad shoved Bait in the chest. Bait tripped over a log and fell down. "Sorry." Brad stepped back, thrust his hands into his pockets. What had gotten into him lately? He couldn't trust himself. He reached out his hand to help Bait up, but the younger boy wiped his hands on his jeans and got up himself.

"You're just sore 'cause we caught you being dumb," he muttered.

"Kids!" Mr. Bates threw up his hands. "Come and eat." He passed out glasses of orange juice. "Drink up, everyone."

Billows of smoke but not much flame rose from the fire. A screaming magpie laughed from the top of the pine tree. Lane came from under the trees carrying a bunch of dry twigs and branches she had snapped off dead trees. The fire caught and roared. Sparks flew twenty feet in the air from one not quite dry poplar branch.

Brad spied Grant and Anna Traynor coming down the

path from the creek, arms entwined, looking like a couple of teenagers who had been necking. People! Traynors, the eternal good scouts, except for Mr. Traynor being stubborn about cars. The Peebles, with their elegant cabin, fancy clothes, and funny kind of formality. And Azim's folks, calling every day to check on their "little lad." Then there were his own parents, so old and set in their ways with his piano and her garden. Brad couldn't remember ever seeing his parents touch each other, let alone walk hand in hand or kiss.

"Toast, Brad." Mrs. Traynor joined him at the campfire, her face flushed from walking. She impulsively put an arm around Brad, giving his shoulder a squeeze. Her hair smelled of wood smoke and soap. He pulled away.

"Sorry." Her hand dropped as if a hot coal had landed on it. "I think of you as one of the family."

He grabbed two slices of bread from the open plastic bag on the table, found a good spot by some red hot embers and held the toasting stick near the orange and yellow glow. *Not a good move, Bradley, pulling away from Mrs. Traynor like that.* He wasn't used to people touching him. She'd taken him by surprise.

First the episode with Bait, then Mrs. Traynor. He should stay away from people if he couldn't handle himself better.

The whole Scout troop stood around the campfire munching, concentrating on food. They didn't seem to know he had a battle going on inside. Human beings must be like volcanoes, erupting suddenly. Most of life went on underneath like lava and hot and cold gases. How do you keep a lid on it? What if people found out what he was really like? He had this huge hunk of darkness and anger inside him and every once in a while it exploded. No one needed a person like that in their group. These good folks wouldn't want him around, hitting his friends, hurting Mrs. Traynor's feelings, if they knew what he was really like. He gnawed his knuckles.

Matt danced around the fire, looking like a sawed-off football player with ants in his pants. He stuffed four slices of toast and jam in his mouth at once. Junk's bread fell in the flames. The smell of burnt toast filled the air. Azim coughed. Ashley Sargent combed her hair and looked bored.

"Cooties, cooties," Tommy Ho ran away.

"Such a child." Ashley sounded like a snob.

Lane, Kenny and Bait helped Mr. Bates tidy up.

"Inspection in thirty minutes," Grant Traynor said. "Meet by the creek in an hour. We've a lot of work to do."

Mrs. Traynor stared at Brad. She looked troubled. He smiled shyly at her and she smiled back; her face cleared. He ran to catch Kenny who was at their new campsite checking things out.

"Good job, Brad, we should win." Kenny tightened one of the ropes holding the fly up.

"Not after last night," Brad snorted.

"So much for trying to cover up." Kenny swept three gum wrappers out of the tent and shoved them in his pocket.

"You can't win 'em all," Brad sighed. *And with my current rate of goofs, I won't win anything.*

"I'd like to, though." Kenny checked the sodden sleeping bags. "These are going to take forever to dry. What will we do tonight?"

"Worrywart."

"Wombat."

"Bradwurst."

"Kennyfried Chuckem."

"Not bad, not bad." Kenny poked Brad in the back with a bony finger. "We've got a food fixation, that's what Auntie

Peebles would say."

"She teaches social studies, not psychology." And Brad remembered his stupid assignment, the family tree. He unfolded the sheet that had been tucked in the top pocket of the knapsack, spread it out on the stump. One dead grandfather, a missing uncle on Desmond's side, two dead grandparents and someone who raised his mom, some aunt on the Clark side. It had to be enough. It was all he had. He couldn't make up the rest, not like Kenny had suggested. It wasn't right. He had to live with what he had.

Brad heaved a sigh and tucked the paper away. He'd give it to Mrs. Peebles on Monday at school. Inside Brad felt cold and hollow, like there was a pit, one so deep and dark he was afraid to look over the edge, or throw a pebble down. Like a black hole in the universe, it drained energy, exerted some gravitational tug. It made him dizzy. He couldn't think of a math problem or a project to cover the panic that welled up. Don't give in to it, Brad, don't give in. He had to stay part of the world, find out who he was and what he could do. No sense getting trapped.

"Okay you guys. Mr. Traynor's inspection team's coming," Azim warned from a branch of an elm. He leapt deftly to the ground.

Brad and Kenny were ready.

"Neat campsite, boys," Grant said. "But your recent history loses you points. Lane and Ashley won the Good Campkeeping Award for the day."

"Figures," Kenny snorted. "But can they build bridges?"

8. THE BRIDGE

BRAD AND LANE, with saws, rope and tape measure, scoured the woods for bridge supports. They were deep in the forest on the far side of the creek. They'd crossed on stones, but both had gotten one foot wet.

"Four inches in diameter, twelve to sixteen feet long." Brad surveyed a dense green stand of poplar. Repeating the dimensions gave him confidence.

"Without bends or big knots," Lane pointed to one light green tree. They both nodded. Lane started sawing two feet from the ground. Brad found another likely candidate and began sawing too. A startled pheasant fluttered up.

"Race?" Lane swept prickly rose bushes away from her bow saw with a leather work glove. She grinned at him, sweat shining on her forehead, damp curls clinging to her cheeks.

"You're on," Brad smiled back. Something about working with Lane made him feel good, better than working alone. First, they made a short cut in the far side, then they sawed from the side nearest them—an inch up from the first cut— sawed right through the trees, aiming them to fall into some raspberry bushes, hoping they wouldn't get hung up in surrounding tree branches. Sweat glistened on Brad's forehead.

Lane's cheeks flushed pink from exertion.

"Timber," hollered Lane.

"Timber," shouted Brad, wiping perspiration from his face with a red cowboy hankie. He tucked it away fast. Trust his mom to buy him cute things. It was embarrassing.

The two trees fell together with a crash and a crackle.

"I love it out here." Brad broke short branches off so it would be easier to drag the tree through the bush.

"Me too." Lane dragged her tree out to the path and began cutting off its branches. "But I wouldn't want such a fancy house. I hate housework. Auntie Peebles thrives on it."

"I'd live mostly outdoors." Brad tied the two trees together with the other two they had felled. "This is enough, with the other four we've gotten."

"We sure scared that pheasant out of his tree," Lane said. "Looked almost as startled as you did when my mom tried to give you a hug."

"She surprised me, that's all." Brad hung his saw over his shoulder.

"Dad says a hug a day keeps the therapist away." Lane looped the rope around her middle and hauled the trees. Brad pulled at the same speed and the two of them made fair progress down the path, leaving a trail of disturbed leaves, clover and strawberry plants.

"Ever since your dad came home you've been having a tough time," Lane said. "Is there some way I can help? Is there something Kenny or I could do?"

Brad gave Lane a puzzled look, and kept pulling. The logs were heavy and the rope cut into his middle. "Nothing."

"Don't give me that." Beads of perspiration rimmed Lane's bushy eyebrows. "What are friends for?"

"I don't know," said Brad as he marched faster, hauling

the logs so quickly away from Lane's probing that his legs ached. Lane groaned as she tried to keep up.

"Take it easy," Lane wheezed, tugging at the ropes that held the two of them together. "You're not alone in this."

"Don't I wish." Brad slowed as they came into the clearing. He shook himself like a wet dog.

"How many logs?" Kenny shouted.

"Bring them over here." Mr. Traynor stood in the middle of the construction site. The plans and the tools were laid out on a picnic table.

Azim and Matt used Peebles' fence-post digger to put the holes in the ground for the eight supports. Ashley and Tommy peeled the logs and applied a coat of creosote to the base. Mr. Bates and his son paced out the distance and checked the survey markers with fluttering orange tapes waving on the tops. A pile of precut 1 x 4s in four-foot lengths sat waiting for a coat of stain. They were making the bridge wide enough for two people walking side by side, or a small garden tractor.

"Ow!" Ashley screamed. "I cut myself."

She dropped the log peeler and clutched her knee. Blood oozed out between her fingers. She toppled over and lay on her side, curled up, moaning. "It's really bad."

"Grab the first aid kit," Grant shouted. Kenny leaped in the back of the van and hauled out the bright blue plastic box.

"Lane, run up to the house and ask your aunt to phone the local doctor. Let her know we're coming." He turned to the pale girl sitting on the ground, rocking back and forth. "Too bad Dr. Peebles had to go to town, I thought we'd have a resident doctor … Let me see it, Ashley, let me see it."

"I hate blood," Ashley cried. "Look at my jeans." The knee of her trousers was stained red.

The kids clustered around. Mr. Traynor knelt before Ashley. He grabbed the scissors from the first aid kit and cut away the matted material. Tommy gasped as blood flowed down Ashley's leg. A flap of loose skin the shape of the blade of the dropped log peeler quivered as Grant mopped blood, trying to see the extent of the wound. "Stand back, kids. Let her breathe."

He took a blue bandana out of his pocket and made a tourniquet above the kneecap. He picked her up, huffing and puffing, and carried her up the hill.

"Why not use the van?" Brad asked.

"Dad left the parking lights on and it won't start. We're recharging the battery up at the house."

Brad shook his head in disbelief. How could Mr. Traynor be so good at bridges and Scouts and teaching and such a klutz in other ways? It didn't make sense.

Mrs. Traynor stood at the top of the hill with the door to the old Honda open and the motor running. "Lane, come with me to keep Ashley company. We have to drive into Camden. The Blueberry Creek doctor's on holidays."

"It will need stitches," said Grant as he helped Ashley into the front seat. Lane climbed in the back. Watching the confusion and Ashley's drawn face Brad felt suddenly helpless and young. His mouth went dry.

"Anything else we need?" Anna Traynor asked.

"Take my sleeping bag and dry it at the laundromat, will you?" Kenny held out his still damp bag. Brad was surprised that his buddy had thought about running down and getting it. He himself had been too overwhelmed by Ashley's accident to think about anything else.

"What about Brad's?" Lane asked.

"He's tougher than me," Kenny shrugged.

"You forgot, you weasel," Lane taunted. "Self-centered kid, that's what you are." She looked Brad's way. She smiled and nodded at him. Brad blushed.

Kenny ran down the hill so fast he rolled the last few meters. He returned huffing and puffing with Brad's bag.

"Take it easy, Anna, the clutch is slipping. Don't forget to pump the brakes." Mr. Traynor waved the little Honda away.

Brad watched the car in its fog of exhaust, putt-putt down the lane and out of sight. He felt abandoned. He'd come to get away from everything that was bugging him and it had followed him. He got angry too easily. He and Kenny looked dumb. The kids thought he was too serious. He felt as if his life was flying apart. And he hadn't been injured like poor Ashley. But when she got cut, it reminded him of all the times he had cut himself. It hurt; he knew what it meant to hurt.

"Camping is always a little dangerous." Mr. Traynor and Brad walked back to the construction site. "There are different rules and we don't remember them easily. At home we do all sorts of things on automatic pilot, but out here you have to think everything through. It pays to take your time."

"I should have spotted that grassy river behind where Kenny and I camped," Brad sighed. "I should have known it would flood if it rained."

"Ashley should have made sure her leg wasn't near the blade," Kenny added.

Brad and Kenny both looked over at Mr. Traynor and then down at the stalled van.

"Oh, yeah, I get it. I should have checked the lights."

Maybe going away with people wasn't such a good idea, Brad thought. You see them too clearly, warts and all. You even see yourself clearly and I don't like what I see.

9. STARGAZING

"HEAVE," MR. BATES called. The last of the uprights for the bridge dropped into place. Sweat streaming into their eyes, bodies straining with effort, Kenny and Brad shoveled dirt into the hole, surrounding the pole with a thick clay and sand mixture. Grant and the other boys were finishing the cross-supports that would hold each pair of logs in place. The bridge would have three spans —a ramp led to the first uprights, eight feet to the uprights closest to the creek, twelve feet to cross the creek—wide enough to span the flow of water even at flood time—and eight feet to the last pair of uprights. Kenny, Brad and Mr. Bates lashed the crosspieces with sturdy ropes.

"Break time!" Mrs. Peebles hollered. She and Tommy Ho came bearing fresh biscuits, tea and juice for everyone. "We've got the railings peeled and painted. The floor supports are dry and ready to nail in place."

"Great shakes! We're sure to be done tomorrow," Kenny crowed. "Wait until Lane sees how far we've gotten."

Brad's brow furrowed. "Shouldn't they be back?"

Grant blew on his hot tea, wiped sweat from his forehead with an already soggy red-patterned kerchief, and stared at his watch. "Maybe Ashley's wound was worse than we thought."

"Maybe they've had an accident," Brad muttered. The beat-up Honda had been jouncing around in his mind all the time he had been working.

"We could use more milk," Mrs. Peebles said. "I'll drive to the corner store and see if there is any sign of them."

"Me too," Matt volunteered. "I could buy Cheezies and chocolate bars."

"It's your turn to lash bridge supports," Kenny said. "I'll go. I'm worried."

Brad ran a dirty hand through his hair. "Why don't I go?"

Azim blew an exaggerated kiss Brad's way. "Sweet on Ashley, are you?"

Brad threw a withering glance at him.

"Brad goes, the rest of you guys get back to work." Grant headed toward the pile of three inch saplings that were going to serve as side pieces. The 1 x 4 slats would be nailed to them, leaving a half-inch gap between each floorboard. Several crosshatches of two-inch saplings would strengthen the spans.

Matt gave Brad five bucks to buy goodies for him.

Mrs. Peebles turned the car radio on. Brad winced. It was playing mall music featuring no-name bands and no-name artists. Enough to put a guy to sleep. They drove in silence down the gravel road, dust clouds filling the air behind the car.

"Good-looking bridge, Brad," Mrs. Peebles said.

Brad nodded. They approached the corner where the Honda had gone off the road yesterday. Brad could see the skid marks. The rest of the trip was uneventful.

A tow truck with the battered Honda attached sat idling in the yard of the garage and store at the junction to the highway.

Brad leapt from the car and ran into the store. Had something happened to Lane, to Mrs. Traynor? His heart squeezed like a chunk of wood held in a vice on his workbench. He threw the screen door open and tripped over a white bucket filled with candy wrappers, orange peels and empty juice cartons.

Everyone in the store turned to stare at him. Smells of candy, sliced luncheon meats and that floor cleaner they use in schools and hospitals assailed Brad as he bent to pick up the debris.

Mrs. Traynor, Lane and Ashley stood around the phone. "Brad's just arrived, made his entrance is more like it." Mrs. Traynor spoke into the phone. "Grant, I tried changing gears going up the hill but they wouldn't work. Then the hand-brake failed and we started rolling backwards. Good thing nothing was coming. We had seat belts and a wide shoulder … The car finally stopped with a thud, I'll tell you, up against a road sign … A truck came barreling down the hill just as we landed. If he had come a few minutes earlier we would have been still in the middle of the road … Where? Right near the Blueberry side road. I called the AMA; the guy wants to know where to take it."

She paused, waved at Brad. Mrs. Peebles shook her head, sighed and went to the counter to buy milk.

"Are you all right," Brad asked the girls. "What happened? How's your knee?" He glanced from Lane to Ashley and back again.

"I needed five stitches." Ashley's eyes sparkled. "You should have seen the doctor who bandaged it up. He was gorgeous."

Lane poked Brad. "All of a sudden Ashley was a pillar of strength, I tell you, Bradley, a pillar of strength."

"You could have been badly hurt." Brad stated flatly. "What if that truck …"

"Yeah, I know. I shouldn't have come on this stupid camping trip. Two accidents and my whole body feels like I've been tossed around," Ashley moaned. "I'll be sore tomorrow. The doctor gave me painkillers."

Brad turned his attention to Lane. He found himself really watching every move Lane made. He was glad she hadn't been hurt.

"Scary stuff." Lane sat on an open crate of canned peas. "The car came to rest by a road sign. That huge truck would have rammed us. I can't believe we walked away in one piece." Her eyes were studying a shelf of canned vegetables and fruit, but it looked to Brad as if she was seeing through them, seeing the truck bearing down on her and Ashley again. She shuddered.

Mrs. Traynor was talking to the store owner and the tow-truck driver. She went back to the phone.

"Okay, Grant, you can pick the car up on your way home tomorrow." She sighed. "What you want to save it for, I don't know."

Brad shook his head. So much for Mr. Traynor. If Brad ever had a family of his own, not that he figured he would if he was an astronomer working all night, but if he did, he'd take good care of them. It takes more than hugs and talking, lots more.

Ashley received scads of sympathy and attention back at the camp site, but only for the first few minutes. Everyone hustled to work on the bridge while she sat on the hillside and read a Sweet Valley High novel, combed her hair, and made comments about the kids working.

Finally, one tired bunch of Scouts gathered by the camp-fire for chili and garlic bread, ice cream and chocolate sauce, and marshmallows roasted, toasted and dropped in the fire.

When Grant called for lights out, Ashley and Lane left right away. The painkillers Ashley had been given were making her sleepy.

Kenny and Brad rescued their dried sleeping bags from the car and stretched out in the tent. Brad had his head stuck outside the flaps, binoculars held to his eyes.

"I'm too tired to sleep," he said.

Kenny pulled his sleeping bag with him so his head hung out the tent flap too.

Brad passed him the glasses. "We're looking north so the Big Dipper is just above the treetops. I was trying to find Jupiter. It should be high in the sky close to where the sun would be if it were daytime."

"There's one really bright star up there with a bunch of little stars around it." Kenny handed the glasses back.

"Those are the four biggest moons of the giant planet." Brad lay still, focusing on the center of the heavens. He rattled on about Io, Europa, Ganymede, and Callisto. "Ganymede is the largest moon in the solar system. It's bigger than Mercury. Jupiter with its moons traveling around it nightly is like a tiny solar system of its own."

Kenny took the glasses and peered at Jupiter. "Will we ever explore that?"

"It's made of dangerous gases and liquid." Brad rolled over and picked a blade of grass to chew. "We'll land on one of the moons and send robots to the planet. Maybe in our lifetime."

"Wow, awesome stuff." Kenny shivered and pulled the bag around his shoulders.

"Are you guys still awake?" Lane's voice came from the

dark. Her flashlight bobbed as she came near. "I can't get to sleep. Ashley's out for the count."

"Let's build up the fire," Brad said. "I'm getting cold."

Lane padded over to their tent.

"What were you staring at?" Lane whispered. She turned off her flashlight and stared up into the sky.

"Jupiter." Kenny pointed to the brightest star in the dark blue sky.

"The biggest, stormiest planet of them all." Brad blushed in the darkness as if his friends could read his mind. Lying there beside Kenny he'd suddenly felt so close to the universe he could reach out and touch the handle of the Dipper. A buzz passed through him like a current of electricity. Here in the country, under the wide prairie sky with a good pair of binoculars and a head stuffed full of facts, time stood still. He and the sky were attached by the cord of darkness. The night sky was so honest and predictable. With enough charts and maps you could plot the passing planets, stars and constellations forever—until they exploded or you died. When he was a famous astronomer, he'd wait with other scientists for the sky to darken over Hawaii or Peru and the huge telescopes to rumble upward, the massive bubble covers to roll back revealing the planets and constellations in details he couldn't even imagine yet. Brad sighed. That was tomorrow. He had to find something to help him get through today and remind him of his future. He needed some way of burying the anger that kept erupting. Looking up, he suddenly had it. He had a plan.

"This winter I'm going to build a telescope," Brad said as the three of them made their way to the dying campfire.

He was getting really cold. His ankles were freezing. Brad looked down. There was a gap of six inches between the bottom of his old jogging pants and his worn socks. He tried to pull the sweats down. That just exposed his middle to the chill air. Geez, was he ever going to stop this growing streak?

"A telescope, eh?" Kenny hurried to catch up with Brad.

"We could help." Lane was nearly running to keep up.

"It's something I have to do myself," Brad bit his lip. "I'll win the Science Fair."

"You just want to get your picture in the paper like Kenny," Lane said. "Prizes don't make you a winner. Pictures don't make you a winner." An unfamiliar tone in Lane's voice made Brad turn to look at her. He couldn't see her clearly. Something was bothering her.

"You sound more like Mom every day, a regular philosopher." Kenny laughed.

"Kids can get serious, smartso,"

"Speak for yourself, fishbreath," Kenny punched her arm. "You've been funny ever since this afternoon. Did you hit your head?"

"It's none of your business, dork. Brothers should be outlawed." She bent to tie up her sneaker. "I didn't realize, until I was lying down in the tent trying to get to sleep, how scared I got this afternoon, okay? I kept seeing that truck coming over the hill. Mom had her head turned trying to find a safe place to stop. For a second I was afraid we might die. So I'm feeling a little strange tonight."

They had reached the campfire.

"We need more branches." Lane headed into the woods, her flashlight bobbing.

Brad pushed a fat stick into the middle of the embers, stirring the fire as if it were a witch's brew in a cauldron. His head hurt. Lane had been scared, scared to death. He could remember being scared badly. Shadows, cast by the tiny flames he had coaxed from the fire pit, bounced and waved across the dark trees, waved in the wind. He remembered being frightened several times in his life, times when his father screamed at him to get out, to go away, to leave him alone, times his father made him feel bad. Desmond had seemed immense then. A dark house filled with plants and glaring adults, strangers pointing accusing fingers and his father going away.

Brad threw his head back and drank in the peaceful sky, the stars in their places, the planets, the moon moving slowly, cutting a swath of light across the treetops.

People, unlike stars, are unreliable. Kids get hurt, get scared. Maybe only the sky was reliable, the planets circling the sun or the moons circling Jupiter. He'd be better off without people. Stick to binoculars, books and projects, Brad, it's safer.

"There," Lane sighed and threw herself down in front of the now-blazing fire. "That's more like it. I feel better now."

"Fires are so friendly," Kenny said.

"Fires kill." Lane tossed a handful of leaves towards the flames. They crackled and their sparks darted like fireflies.

"Boy, you're depressing," Kenny said. "I was feeling great. Work on the bridge is really coming along."

"Wonder how the 2nd Scouts are doing?" Brad tossed a branch back onto the flames.

"And the Venturers." Kenny poked a stick into the flames, watching the tip burn.

"Does your dad really know what he's doing? Will we win?" Brad asked.

"That's what bugs me about you guys." Lane leaned back against a log. "I hate competition. All the time, marks, grades, points, winners, losers. It turns games into work."

"There you go, sounding like Mom again," Kenny snorted.

"That's what life's like."

"I don't have to like it, do I?" Lane tossed a handful of grass at him. "People aren't robots. Push a button and they perform. People are all different. That's neat."

Brad shook his head. "Without people the world might be a better place."

"Wow, talk about depressed," Lane whistled.

"I've never thought about it." Brad backed off. This was private stuff.

"It's one hot topic at our house," Kenny said. "Should schools push competition? Should kids get marks or grades?"

"Some days it's sickening," Lane admitted. "Talk talk talk."

"We don't talk about stuff much," Brad said. Maybe his dad talked to his therapist in the city. He had appointments every couple of weeks. Brad's mom always had to remind him to go.

"Weird, man," Lane giggled, sounding like some TV character. "What do you do?"

"Nothing. Dad plays the piano. Mom gardens or sells houses, and I do my paper route and build."

"Don't you have dinner conversations?" Lane asked. "We have to talk about our day and the news or something. Mom and Dad don't agree on anything, so we end up sitting there for ages."

Brad couldn't remember when he and his folks had had a conversation about anything. Maybe his mom and dad talked after he'd gone to bed. "My dad talks at people. My mom only talks when she's working."

"Our mom and dad are always talking. That or hugging and junk," Kenny said.

"You got a funny family, Brad," Lane laughed. "Don't your folks get cuddly on the couch?"

"Get out the candlelight and good clothes," Kenny giggled and rolled on the ground. "Spicy perfume and aftershave and a bottle of good wine."

"My folks are too old for that," Brad said. "They have separate bedrooms."

"Separate bedrooms," Lane laughed. "You've got to be kidding. Nobody has separate bedrooms."

"Maybe they sneak together late at night." Kenny waved a long stick above the fire letting the sparks swirl.

Brad pushed himself away from the fire. Desmond and Una May weren't the best folks in the world but they were all he had. He stood up and tossed the stick he'd been poking the fire with onto the flames.

"I'm going to bed," he said.

Kenny and Lane gazed at each other and shrugged their shoulders. They both stood.

"Getting too close to the bone, eh, Brad?" Lane came over to him. "That's what friends are for. Everyone needs someone to share stuff with."

"I don't." Brad turned on his heel and walked back to the tent. He burrowed into his sleeping bag and rolled toward the far corner. Why had coming out here with his friends raised so many questions he couldn't answer, brought back memories that hurt as much as cuts? He wished he could wake in his own bed, follow his own safe patterns, deliver his papers, build models, think about the universe. Brad lay curled quiet as a mouse as Kenny slipped into the tent.

"Brad," Kenny whispered. "Brad?"

Brad didn't answer.

10. THE CONTEST

THE NEXT MORNING Blueberry Creek echoed with the sound of hammers and the splash of water as three of the Scouts, up to their knees in the slow current, lashed crosspieces to the walkway. A mule deer leapt toward the dark and silent woods. The smell of musk and the sight of fallen golden leaves the size and brilliance of dollar coins hinted of winter. Voices called and sang, ricocheting across the valley and up the cliff behind the creek.

Were you ever in Quebec,
stowing timber on a deck,
where there's a king with a golden crown,
riding on a donkey.

Kenny and Brad nailed the 1 x 4" planks to one end of the bridge. Tommy Ho and Lane hammered them down on the other end. They were racing for the middle. Two Senior Scoutmasters from another region were expected after lunch. They were going to inspect Grant's troop, the 2nd Scouts' project, and another project done by the Venturers' troop from Pigeon Lake.

"Move it, move it," Mr. Traynor coached in a cheery voice

as he and Mr. Bates cleaned up the construction site. Mrs. Traynor and Ashley sat on blankets on the hillside watching as the work was finished.

"Phone for Azim," Mrs. Peebles shouted from the porch.

Azim raced from under the middle span of the bridge and up the hill.

"What's going to happen when you go to camp and they can't talk to you every day?" Matt laughed.

"Leave him alone," Lane shouted. "We all have parents to put up with."

Trust Lane, Brad thought as he hammered again. She had people on the brain. With a dad who was great at some things and an absolute failure at others, she had her hands full. Brad hit the board so hard the hammer bounced and wrenched his wrist. He missed the nail.

"Only four more to go," Kenny cheered.

"We've got five," Tommy Ho hollered.

"Count down," Mr. Traynor bellowed like a marine sergeant. "Five, and tell us when. What a great team you are."

"Four," shouted Lane. "I don't know why I let myself in for this," she stage whispered. "Fathers."

"Three," Brad yelled.

Two," Tommy Ho screamed.

"One more board to go," Kenny banged two nails on his side. Brad did the same.

"The inspectors, the inspectors." Azim came flying down the hill, "The Scoutmasters are driving in the lane."

"What did the boy say?" Kenny giggled.

"I said …" Azim began.

"We know, we heard you," Lane said softly. "It's Kenny trying to be funny with emphasis on the word 'trying.'"

Everyone scurried. Scraps of lumber, bark strips, shavings went by the fire pit. By the time the two Scoutmasters walked over the hill, the kids were grinning from ear to ear.

Dr. and Mrs. Peebles came, too. Mrs. Peebles waved a length of red satin ribbon; Dr. Peebles carried a pair of garden shears. They were dressed in matching safari suits the shade of desert sand with Tilley hats and scarves. Their bush jackets had pockets with flaps, watch pockets, pockets with zippers. Their perfume and after-shave bore traces of steamy jungle and tropical flowers. The dishevelled Scouts gawked at the splendor.

Brad's stomach was tied in knots as the two men inspected the bridge. Meanwhile Mrs. Peebles tied the ribbon across the entrance closest to the house. Mr. Bates took photos. Ashley, hobbling dramatically, leaned against the railing. Mr. Traynor strutted with the inspectors as they discussed the relative strength, the load bearing factors, and peered at the lashing, poked at the crosspieces and supports on the uprights.

"I declare the bridge over Blueberry Creek open." The senior Scoutmaster cut the ribbon and led the troop across the bridge single file, Ashley Sargent limping slowly in the rear. They turned and walked back. "And the project complete."

"Rendezvous at the provincial park at 2:30." The two inspectors marched up the hill and disappeared.

"Okay kids, let's pack it in," Grant said.

"Photo first," Mr. Bates said. Everyone lined up, jostled for position. Azim, Brad and Junk ended up in the back row. "Tall for your age, aren't you?" Junk drawled, poking Azim in the ribs.

"My uncle Mohammed is six-foot-five, plays basketball for the university team," Azim answered.

"Say cheese, please," Mr. Bates clicked away.

"What's he like?" Brad asked.

"Who?"

"Your uncle."

Azim looked like he might say more but changed his mind. "He's okay."

Brad nodded. He understood not wanting to talk sometimes. He understood that well.

"What are our chances?" Kenny asked, as the kids broke free from the photo session.

"Of?" Brad asked.

"Of winning, bradwurst."

"I don't know, Kennybunkport." Brad shoved Kenny into the rosebush by the path.

"I'm proud of you, troop." Mr. Traynor stood arms akimbo, feet apart on the bridge approach. "You did your best, that's what counts."

"Winning's what matters." Brad trudged toward their tent.

"My dad," Kenny sighed as they folded the tent, rolled the sleeping bags. "He thinks life's simple. I hate to disillusion him."

"When I was a little kid," Brad said. "I thought life was simple."

"Dad's always bugging me to take it easy, stop worrying so much, stop pushing so hard." Kenny sat back on his heels. "I don't know how."

"Me, either."

"I like a new challenge. Maybe we're outgrowing Scouts. Or I'm outgrowing my dad."

"Next year we should take up whitewater rafting or kayaking. What do you say?" Brad spoke slowly. Maybe he could keep a friend. As long as no one found out what he was really like.

"There's a Voyager Club in the Senior High."

"Sounds great."

As they carried their camping gear to the van Brad looked over his shoulder at the finished bridge. From a distance it looked pretty good. He hoped it was good enough. That wasn't true, he was counting on it being good. Both he and Kenny liked winning. Too bad about Kenny's father. Brad was really disappointed in him. *You should talk, Brad*, he said to himself, *you should talk. What about your dad?*

He stared across the ravine to the horizon. If it weren't for the sun, he would be able to see the planets and constellations on their journeys. The school library had a book by Terence Dickinson called *Exploring the Sky by Day* that he wanted to read. There never seemed to be enough time to do everything he wanted to do. Tonight he would refasten his binoculars to their mount and peer at the sky to his heart's content.

The Traynor van towing the beat-up Honda followed the Bates' station wagon into the provincial park. The other troops shouted as they played a game of touch football. The kids climbed out of the cars and sprinted to join the fray or watch from the sidelines.

Lane and Ashley hung back. Brad sat on the floor of the van lacing his sneakers, picking stray pine needles and burrs from his socks.

"I'm not going over there," Ashley said.

"Come on, it's just a bunch of kids," Lane tugged at her arm.

"You go," Ashley stood her ground. "You're the one that wants to be a Scout. The boys laugh at us. Especially guys from other troops."

"Don't be a wimp, Ashley," Lane pleaded.

"Look, maybe I'm not cut out for this," Ashley shook her

blond hair. "Mom says it's time I grew up."

"What's that mean? You don't think building a bridge is grown up, you don't think I'm grown up." Lane pushed the dirt with the toe of her shoe. "I don't get it."

"I don't know; if I did I'd tell you," Ashley bit her lip and looked away. "Joining Scouts seemed like a good idea. And your mom, she's neat, she's not, you know, weird. I mean she has fun, you know what I mean."

"No, I don't know what you mean." Lane squinted in the sunlight.

Ashley pulled her hand away from Lane's and walked over to a picnic table and sat down. "Just forget it, okay," she said. "My knee hurts."

Brad jumped from the van, startling Lane. She was staring after Ashley with a hurt look on her face.

"Leave her be. It's a phase," Brad said. He jogged to the playing field. Mrs. Peebles, carrying a jug of juice and a stack of plastic glasses, walked over to the picnic table where Ashley sat, her shoulders hunched, her skin paler than pear juice.

The troops lined up. Brad and Kenny inspected their ragtag group. Tommy Ho had a scratched knee with a dirty hankie tied around it. Azim had lost one sock. Bait looked like he had slept in his shirt. Matt was nibbling on cookies and Junk, eyelids drooping as usual, slouched, hands in pockets. Lane raced down the hill and stood beside her mother. The two of them stood together, shoulders straight, facing forward, looking more like two sisters than a mother and daughter.

Brad watched them and wondered briefly, the thought dancing through his head quicker than a butterfly, whether it would have been better for a girl in his family, whether a girl could have made his mother happy and his father proud.

He didn't know, and it wasn't the way life was, so he let the speculation fly away.

The three troops lined up side by side. Trevor and the 2nd Scouts were to the right of Mr. Traynor's troop and the Venturers with their leaders stood to the left. The regional Scoutmaster stepped to the front and cleared his throat.

"I want to compliment all the boys, pardon me, and the girls," he nodded at Ashley sitting off to the side with Mrs. Peebles, then at Lane and two girl Venturers. "On the work they have done."

Brad caught Kenny's eye and gestured with thumbs up.

"The award for the fall project goes to the Venturers from Pigeon Lake. Second place to the 1st Scouts from Camden and third place to the 2nd Scout Troop."

The pit in Brad's stomach opened again. He clamped his mouth shut and clenched his jaw. He didn't hear another word the Scoutmaster said. So much for teamwork and how great they were, let alone how wise Mr. Traynor was. He, Brad, was as much to blame as anyone, and he hated that. They should have won. He knew they could have. The fall sunshine did not stop him from shivering.

As soon as they were dismissed he headed to the outhouse to see this incredible prizewinning entry. Kenny and Lane raced after him.

"It's not so hot." Kenny circled the cedar building. He opened the door and closed it again.

Meanwhile Brad poked and prodded the whole building. Buffalo biscuits, it was good. It was well designed and spacious, the pit was deep. He shone his flashlight down the hole to see how the sides were supported. By four by fours. It was more polished than the bridge. More finishing details. The sharp smell of waterproof stain made him sneeze.

Lane leaned against a birch tree plucking rose thorns from her sleeve. "Live and learn."

"Shut up," Brad shouted. His face was blotchy like he had a fever.

"Don't talk to my sister like that," Kenny retorted.

"Bratwurst hates being a loser," Lane shouted back. "Thinks he's alone. Thinks the rest of us don't care."

"Poor loser," Kenny taunted. "What a loser-face!"

"I wouldn't talk," Brad stormed down the path. "Your whole family is a bunch of losers." He felt dizzy. He reached out and touched a birch tree, leaned his hand on the warm smooth bark, solid as a house. "Leave me alone. Just leave me alone."

In the car going home the kids were subdued, like a hockey team in a four-game slump. Some slept, some stared out the window. Brad sat up straight, holding his shoulders away from Azim and Kenny.

"Better luck next time," Grant said. "Live and learn."

Lane shot a withering glance at her father.

Kenny tried to start a conversation. "What about that family tree assignment, Brad? It's due tomorrow."

Brad didn't answer.

"Brad needs to borrow some relatives. His folks have a secret past."

Brad glared at Kenny and said nothing.

"You could have some of mine," Azim chuckled. "My family tree looks like a rain forest, what with relatives in India, Hong Kong, Australia and Canada."

Brad stared out the window. He'd just hand in what he had and it was nobody's business. Last time he'd tell Kenny anything. Last time he'd tell anyone.

As they drove into town, the street lights of Camden

flashed on, welcoming them.

"Chan's papers are lying on the porch," Kenny said.

"An invitation for burglars." Azim rubbed sleep from his eyes.

"They didn't tell me they were going away," Brad said. "At least Buckles delivered them. That's one less thing to worry about." He was staring down the block at his house, clenching his fists.

A police car was parked in Greaves' laneway. A vague frightening memory leapt from the dark of his childhood. He did not pursue it.

"Out you get, Brad," Grant said. "Hey, hope there's no trouble."

"Want us to wait?"

"No, thanks." Brad slammed the door, hauled his gear up the walk. His head was throbbing. Not again. This was all he needed. A gust of wind whipped a willow branch across his chest as he moved down the cement to the rear of the house. He shoved it away. His throat and chest tightened as if held by ropes.

His mother's face appeared at the back door, holding open the storm door, the glass rattling in the wind. "It's all right, Brad, it's nothing. One of the farms I'm trying to sell was broken into."

Brad dropped his duffel and his pack on the sidewalk. He was exhausted. His arms ached, and he stretched them toward his mother like storm-wracked branches on a young sapling. He reached for her, his mouth open as if he would say something.

His mother stood still, looking uncomfortable, her arms protecting her body from any invasion by linking themselves across her middle.

Brad dropped his arms by his side. The darkness within enfolded him.

"It's fine, Brad. Your dad is fine," his mother said, turning slowly back to the kitchen, wiping her hands on a floury apron. "Des has found a job in the city. Found a job playing piano. We'll be all right."

Brad could hear the overworked motor of the Traynors' van as it disappeared around the corner with its cumbersome load, the dead Honda. His mother had gone back to kneading biscuits, humming the melody of the piece his father was playing in the far room. Brad hugged his sleeping bag tight, close to his chest, so close to his face that he could smell the waxy scent of canvas, rope and nylon. He hugged his belongings to himself as if they were part of him, as if they were all he had in the world.

The heavy smell of geraniums filled the house. Brad lumbered up the stairs to his room. He closed the door.

He was alone and he had decided it was better that way. He would concentrate on important things—his telescope, and perhaps a computer game for kids—to enter in the Spring Fair.

11. NIGHT CALL

"BRAD'S STUCK UP," Ashley whispered. It was several months later. "Thinks he's better than all of us." Lane had asked Brad if he was coming with them for treats after Scouts one cold December night.

Brad pulled his ski jacket hood over his ears, shoved his hands in his pockets and walked away. "I've got homework," he muttered.

Not true. He wanted to glue the plywood tube of his telescope together. He only had a couple of hours a night to work. Finding directions for building a telescope that he could understand, buying and transporting the plywood, bugging the lumber yard for scraps of Teflon and a sink cutout of formica, ordering the six-inch mirror, coaxing his dad to pick up a couple of movie cans from a camera store in the city to use for bearings, and then the slow process of assembling had eaten up much of the fall. While he searched for materials, or glue dried, he worked on other projects for the Spring Fair—star maps, a diorama, and a video game on stargazing for kids. Brad did his paper route, went to school, did his chores around the house, and went to Scouts once a week.

He had had no time for friends, not since the camping

fiasco. He'd stuck to business, the business of becoming a winner. He had decided he didn't need friends, unless you counted Orion, the hunter. Each night, after Brad had changed out of his carpentry jeans and shirt, he bundled in jacket and mitts and stepped onto his balcony to greet the brightest star cluster in the clear northern sky. The constellation was formed by three stars as the belt, two for Orion's shoulders and two for his knees or sword depending on whose map you followed.

Brad trained his binoculars on the Orion Nebula, just below Orion's belt. New stars were buried in the clouds of gas and dust. A baby star nursery, one astronomy book had called it, only 1,500 light years away. His mind played with the familiar facts like they were warm marbles in a jean's pocket.

Stars are formed from gas and dust. The debris of the universe comes together to create the new. This all happened long ago and far away. We human beings are frail tiny bundles of stardust, and yet we get caught up in day-to-day struggles while the universe rolls past our window. We lose perspective.

"I don't think I'm better, whatever Ashley says," Brad whispered to the cold wind that crackled branches in the elm tree, blew a trash can lid down the lane. "I don't. I need a space of my own. Like out here on the threshold of the universe. Besides, I want to finish something right. Real friends would understand that."

He slid the door to the balcony shut, threw his jacket and clothes on the bulgy brown chair and climbed into bed. He stared at the dark ceiling. He would like Kenny to see what he was building. Compare notes. He did miss Lane poking into his life. Maybe being alone all the time wasn't so great.

Later he slid into a recurring nightmare. He was on a spacecraft and he couldn't find any other crew, not by opening doors or peering through windows. He ran down long corridors, but he didn't get anywhere. It was as if he were running in slow motion. Police sirens wailed in the background. His father and mother sat together on a park bench near a fountain, maybe on a holograph deck. He motioned to them, pleaded with them to come with him, but it was as if they couldn't see him. Up ahead a door opened, a gantry swung out, and he, in a space suit, was flung out, a double coil of cord unravelling with him as he hurtled into darkness, past space debris, past tumbling meteorites, his breath sucked from him like juice through a straw. His body collapsed into his bones.

Brad woke with a start, the phone ringing. He lay listening, returning from his dream, trying to recapture his body. His mother's voice sounded half-asleep and choked.

"When did it happen?"

Brad tiptoed to the door. He didn't open it but stood so close he could smell the printer's ink on his poster of *Worlds in Collision*. His father was whispering.

"When's the funeral? Will you go? How long will you stay? How much will it cost?"

"Was she in pain?" His mother's voice was like stardust on the surface of the earth, heavy beyond description. She must be twirling the cord of the telephone around her fingers nervously, because Brad could hear its clicking faintly against the table. "I'll take the morning bus."

Silence and listening and his father's slippers padding to the bathroom, the water running.

"No, you needn't worry, I'll come alone," Una Greaves sighed.

The receiver clunked on its cradle. His father came shuffling back.

"She was an old woman, Una."

"She was all I had left."

"You need tea." His father's voice was soft, unfamiliar. "I'll make tea, will I?"

"I need to pack. Her bridge partner found her. She was lying in the middle of the living room floor, her purse clasped in her hand, her hat on."

"Belle was like that." Desmond whistled through his teeth. "No one wears hats nowadays."

"What will we tell Bradley?"

"He's a self-centered child. Children don't care about old people. What he doesn't know won't hurt him. I don't believe in all this modern psychology, discussing everything with children. What do they know ..."

"Oh, Desmond." His mother sounded exasperated. "I haven't time for one of your lectures. It's too late now. I wish I'd taken him to visit her more often, to visit his Great Aunt Belle."

Brad's door creaked as he leaned his head against it.

"Shush, you'll wake him." The third step groaned as his father headed downstairs.

"I should have taken him ..." Brad's mothers' voice faded as she followed his father down the steps.

"No, Una, it's better this way." There was a finality in his father's tone. The upstairs hallway stilled. The darkness in Brad's room became oppressive as a cave.

Brad hunkered against the door, his body curled like a baby in a crib. He wanted to scream and strike out. All his muscles jerked in spasms. A dust ball, disturbed by his collapse, rose in the air and fell again. So much for pouring hours and days into projects and entries for the Fair, making star maps and losing oneself in the night sky. He was a child. He was self-centered and the less he knew the better.

And somewhere his Great Aunt Belle whom he could dimly remember, lay dead, wearing a hat, clutching an old woman's purse.

White light shone through the window. Streaks of moonlight crossed the floorboards and Brad wished he could ride one of them over to Kenny's and Lane's and play Risk or work on a jigsaw puzzle or have Mrs. Traynor ruffle his hair. He shivered, wrapped his arms around himself and fell into bed.

The moon drifted behind a cloud. The aurora borealis, the northern lights, lit up the sky, waves and sheets of light particles dancing and billowing in the dark, curtains of faint green and blue shimmering like ghosts, appearing and disappearing, first in one quadrant of the sky, then another. A cosmic light show. Splendor weaving across the sky and no one to see it except him. Tears gathered in the corners of his eyes.

An old woman dies and the atmosphere of the Earth lights up. Perhaps the universe celebrates and sorrows. Brad hoped so. He clung to that thought more tightly than his pillow. Drum's dog howled. Then a stray cat keened like a woman mourning a loved one. Brad slept.

☆

"Where are you going?" Brad flew down the stairs, tucking his shirt in, running his fingers through untidy hair.

His mom and dad were hurrying out the front door, his mom's face red and blotchy like she had a fever.

"Oh, Brad," she spread her arms like a singer. "Aunt Belle died." Her hands fell to her sides.

"There's a note on the kitchen table," his father said brusquely. "You don't want to miss the bus, Una May."

"She was going to play bridge. She had her hat and gloves on. Eighty-three, she was eighty-three in October. Heart, it was heart."

Brad's dad pushed Una into the passenger seat like she was a reluctant child. He darted to the driver's side, tossing the suitcase into the back seat.

"She raised me, you know. I always meant you to know her better, Bradley." Her eyes seemed out of focus, glancing back at him as the car pulled out. Her mouth formed words even as the car sped away.

Brad watched the billows of exhaust hover in the driveway, heard the tires crunch on fresh snow, felt the tingle of flakes on his cheeks. He waved.

"Safe trip." Brad spoke to the cold gray air that lowered the sky to the rooftops.

He bundled up to deliver his papers, checked his pockets for mitts. Stupid kid, there was a wad of *Journal* money that he'd forgotten to put in his room. Mr. Drum had paid for his papers last night. So had Mrs. Chan. After Brad paid the *Journal* guy his share, he'd have thirty-two dollars to add to his fund for science projects, trips and university. He'd have to work hard. "Wonder if there's a university in Mom's hometown?" he asked Drum's dog as he struggled against the wind, pulling a sleigh full of daily papers.

The dog didn't answer. The air in front of his long snout fogged with ice crystals as he padded patiently beside Brad.

"I should nickname you Sirius after the dog star. That's the brightest star in the constellation Canus Major, Orion's big dog. You hang close enough. Sirius, now, he's 8.6 light years from here."

Cold wind struck Brad's cheeks like flint on stone, creating a mixture of heat and cold. He whistled as he delivered the news quickly, running up walks, folding papers to put them in mailboxes or in between storm doors and solid oak front doors. Funny, he felt more alive this morning than he had for months. Was it the phone call? He could see that old lady with her hat and gloves, and hear his mother's sad voice. She had become real to him on the day of her death. It was hard to mourn someone you couldn't remember well. Losing someone you love must really hurt. Poor mom.

Like the cutting wind on his face, life had wakened him. There were people out there who cared about him and he was missing them. He couldn't hide in his room forever. He raced the dog to Chan's, dropped the paper between the doors and ran home pulling the clattering sleigh behind him, like a pony with a wagon galloping across a field just for the fun of it.

His father was sitting in the dark kitchen sipping coffee. Brad flipped on the light.

"Mom catch the bus?" He got down hot cereal and a pot to cook it in. He glanced around the kitchen for the note. It was gone.

His father nodded, took another sip of coffee and cleared his throat. "Your mother wanted me to tell you about Aunt Belle."

There was another pause.

Brad stirred the oatmeal into the boiling water, added a little salt and a pinch of cinnamon. He clapped the lid on it, turned the heat down and sat across from his dad, nursing a tall glass of milk.

"We used to live there."

"Where? Saskatchewan?"

"Before Saskatchewan. In B.C." His father stood so quickly the chair nearly tipped. He poured himself another cup of coffee. It slopped on the counter. He mopped it carefully and hung the wash rag over the tap.

"About Aunt Belle." Brad prodded. "We lived in B.C.?"

"Killop, B.C. We lived in Killop in the house next door." Desmond sipped coffee. He walked to the window looking out at the falling snow for help. "I've got a lot of work to do today. I have to practise for my Christmas performances at the hotel."

"But mom said …"

His father pulled himself straight as an arrow and walked toward the music room. "Let's just say your mother's family were unsympathetic. Something happened. It was blown out of proportion. We left." His next words came in a rush like runoff after a storm. "Aunt Belle Clark raised Una May after her folks were killed in an accident on the Trans-Canada highway. She was five and her face was jammed into the rear view mirror. It took five operations to repair the damage."

Brad drained his glass of milk, thirsty suddenly for more.

"She was older than me with a crooked face when I met her. Lived at home. Loved music. She had a beautiful soprano voice. Beautiful." He rubbed his hands together in a washing motion. "I told her you didn't need to know all this. I told her."

The door to the music studio opened and closed. Brad sat alone at the table in the spotless kitchen. Soon, songs of the 1950s came cascading from the keys. The bass hand heavy as if his father was pushing the chords through the floor.

The lid on the oatmeal rattled. Brad poured the steaming porridge into the bowl, added great heaps of brown sugar and cold milk. He blew on each spoonful before carrying it to his mouth.

Slowly, ever so slowly, he was piecing his history together. Curiosity killed the cat; what would it do to boys who want to know? I want to know everything. What makes the world go around? What made the universe? Where do I come from?

He thought of Lane. She was a better psychologist than Lucy in Charlie Brown cartoons. Not that he'd tell her his problems. They weren't problems as much as puzzles he wanted to solve. Just hanging around her and Kenny again would be good. He'd missed them more than he'd expected to. He wanted to see what Kenny had built.

His Great Aunt Belle in Killop, B.C., died last night. His mother's face was hurt in the accident that killed her parents.

"Blue moon, I saw you standing alone, without a dream in your heart, without a love of your own." His father's true tenor voice floated through the house. His accompaniment was gentle like spring rain.

Brad rinsed his bowl under the tap, let the warm water run over his hands until a faint mist rose from the sink to fill the kitchen with humid air. He took the money from his jacket pocket and carried it upstairs to his room and put it in his cash box. He gathered his homework, tiptoed down the stairs and let himself out the back door, clicking the knob so it locked. His father could be lost to the world for hours, singing and playing with no one to interrupt him.

12. CLIMBING BACK ON

AS BRAD TRUDGED down the street to school he kicked toefuls of old snow from the shoveled banks onto the cleared sidewalks.

Old Drum stuck his head out the door. "Don't do that, boy. I just cleaned the walk."

Brad shook his head. He shifted his sports bag from one hand to the other and waved at the old man. Poor guy living alone with his dog. Must get lonely. "Sorry, sir," he shouted.

"Unconscious. I've seen you, staying up too late staring at the night sky," Drum chuckled. His dog pawed the storm door. It opened a crack. Brad could hear Drum scold the dog. The old man used the same tone he'd used to scold Brad. The red tail, waving like a plume on an old-fashioned hat, disappeared into the warm little house. Brad envied the setter and wanted to run after him, follow the old dog into the well-lit house.

Brad slowed outside Traynors'. A beautiful Christmas wreath hung on the door, blue lights covered the blue spruce. The cat meowed. Brad thought about stopping but he saw a new red Honda parked in the driveway. They must have company. Maybe relatives. No place for him, coming in, coming back like he wanted.

The garage door opened automatically and Mr. Traynor came striding out, a bunch of keys jiggling in his hand. "Hey, Brad, fancy seeing you here. How do you like it?"

Brad shoved his hands in his pockets.

"I took your advice." Grant patted the hood of the car, sweeping off the light dusting of snow. "I'm even planning on cleaning out half of the garage so we can put this baby away."

Brad crunched up the lane to the car. "It's great."

"Want a ride to school?"

Brad looked toward the house.

"Lane and Kenny are coming at the last minute." Mr. Traynor stretched across the front seat and opened the passenger door. "Big stars in the afternoon concert."

"Oh," Brad bit his lip. His best friends and he'd forgotten they were in the concert. He was singing in the chorus. His mom and dad had been planning on coming. His mom missed teaching so much she wanted to see the little kids perform, she said. His dad didn't say why he was coming. Maybe with her away he'd stay home.

After supper the two Scout troops were going on a hay ride. Not Brad, though. Freezing his butt on some dumb horse-drawn wagon across the cold prairie hadn't sounded like much fun.

"Is there still room for me on the hay ride tonight?" he asked as they pulled into the school parking lot.

"Sure," Grant beamed. "I thought you were mad at us or something, kid." Grant locked the doors and checked the hatchback. "Thought you might be disappointed in us— losing the Scout project, the old car hassle, you and Kenny building your campsite in a dry creek bed."

Brad shivered as if someone had walked over his grave.

"I've been busy. I've been building a telescope and projects for the Science Fair."

"And passing more badges in three months than any other Scout I've seen." Grant put his arm around Brad's shoulder. Brad did not pull away this time and the two of them walked to the school door together. "What's chasing you, Brad? A ghost? Why don't you take it easy on yourself? Have some fun. All work and no play …"

"Makes Brad a dull boy," Brad finished the sentence. Mr. Traynor went striding down the brightly lit hallway with its murals, poems, Christmas decorations, Holiday greetings. It reminded Brad for a moment of his mother's indoor jungle. Winters, Una May brought as many plants as she could indoors. The house was steamy with growing things, noisy with music. Now the school was filled with boughs and trees and poinsettias and hay and paper maché donkeys and camels. Where could he go?

He went to the library. The librarian had told him she had a new book that talked about what the star over Bethlehem might have been. He found it on the New Books display, took it to a table and began reading.

"Did you see our new car?" Kenny nudged Brad as they put on their gym shoes. "It's got a tapedeck and everything."

"What happened to the old Honda?" Brad asked.

"Sold it to the wreckers." Kenny moved off. Brad followed him, talking.

"My mom's gone away."

"Where?"

The rest of the class barreled past. Buckles stopped to tie

up his laces. The teacher wouldn't let them run in gym with their shoelaces untied. "If it isn't my two favorite goody-goody boys," he snarled.

Brad ignored him and went on talking to Kenny. "My Great Aunt Belle died in Killop, B.C. That's where I lived when I was a little kid."

"That's where we're from, good old Killop, B.C." Buckles hurried to catch up to his cronies. "Maybe we're related, Bradley, wouldn't that be terrible?" He made a fist and punched the air in front of Brad's face.

"Boys!" Mr. Mason called.

Kenny ran beside Bradley to the end of the gym. They did three laps. Brad could feel Kenny's eyes on him as if he was trying to figure something out. Maybe he should say something.

"It said in the paper that there could be more universes than ours. Tons more galaxies than we ever imagined," Brad announced.

☆

In the afternoon the parents came for coffee, sandwiches and the concert. Brad's dad came in and had difficulty finding a chair. Desmond Greaves looked out of place, uncomfortable.

Finally Mr. Traynor, who had been organizing things back stage, went over and visited with Brad's dad. Kenny joined them. Brad, sitting in his white shirt and new longer gray flannels on the hard stacking chair, felt his toes itching in his new size eleven leather shoes.

They had trouble getting the children collected in class units and teachers ran to and fro. The principal stood nervously by the podium.

"They should have done the juice and cookies after instead of before," Brad reflected.

"But some of the parents were late because of work," the kid beside him said. "My mom couldn't come until 4:30. Her boss wouldn't let her."

Now Lane and Mrs. Traynor joined the gathering around Desmond Greaves. Brad's father looked happier, waving his spidery arms telling a story. He flipped long hair from his eyes and smiled at the Traynors. Brad turned away as the principal cleared his throat, the lights flashed on and off twice and the production got underway.

Kenny's piano solos came after the choir sang two carols and "Frosty the Snowman." Lane, Ashley and three Sixth Graders did a lip-sync, air-guitar version of a Madonna song. Lane had the best rhythm. Ashley Sargent kept flinging her long waves about. She was turning more precious every day. Watching a girl choose to be a Barbie doll was a bummer. Thank goodness Lane was still human.

After the concert Brad found his dad on the front steps of the school talking to Kenny and Mrs. Traynor. "The boy has real talent, Anna. Too bad I don't teach children anymore. He reminds me of myself when I was young." Desmond ruffled Kenny's hair.

Brad shuddered, the well opening inside, an unexplained fear bubbling up.

"Time to go home, Dad," Brad said. He started down the steps.

"See you later?" Kenny asked. "Want to stop on your way to the church hall?"

"No, I've got a few last minute collections for my paper route."

"Right." Kenny's voice was shrill.

"Your choir went sharp on the first piece and flat on the second." Desmond Greaves' long strides took him past Bradley on the sidewalk. "When I led children's choirs, I never let them get into bad habits."

Brad took two steps to his father's one to catch up. Then he kept astride. His legs were getting longer. Soon he would be taller than his dad. He grinned at the thought. The air in front of his face fogged.

"Of course, the music teacher hasn't the skill. My choirs won awards. My students were prizewinners. I'd give my right arm to get my hands on Kenny Traynor." His dad's round dark eyes glistened in the street light.

Brad shuddered. "I'm building a telescope for the Science Fair."

"Why don't you bring your friends over to the house more often?" Dad turned down their street. "We could have a musical evening."

"I've gotten six new badges since October," Brad said.

"I'd like to give Kenny some little compositions I made especially for my best students."

"Grandpa's binoculars are really great," said Brad as he unlocked the front door. "Were you in Scouts too?"

"Me, well, I didn't have time for knots and little boy's games, Bradley. I was going to be a concert pianist but ..."

The story went on as they hung up their coats. Brad went through to the kitchen and started cracking eggs into a bowl, smashing two in the process. He picked flecks of eggshell out of the mixture before he beat the omelet and poured it into the frying pan. It sizzled in the melting butter. Brad's chest was tight. I'm a big boy, he told himself, blinking his eyes furiously. Something inside was pushing him. Even if finding out about his roots was going to hurt he wanted to do it. He needed to know. Even dumb old Rory Buckholz knew about his past.

Stargazing was easy. Building a telescope was hard work, but it went step by step, following the instructions. It took time and patience. Knowing facts was fun, inventing things was great, but it wasn't enough. Piecing together your history, your life took longer.

His father was playing the piece Kenny had performed. Only he was playing it better. He was sitting alone in his studio playing the piano. Desmond didn't seem to know what to do without Mom there. She took care of the practical things. Brad folded cheddar cheese into the omelet. He watched it bubble, flipped it and set the table for two. Maybe if he'd been musical ...

The buzzer on the stove went. The toast popped.

"Supper's ready, Dad," Brad said. "Come and get it."

They ate in silence.

"Come on, Bradley," Ashley patted the seat beside her on the hay wagon. She giggled. She was wearing lipstick, and pink eye shadow to match her pink fluffy ski suit. Her white boots had pink tassels.

"I thought you quit Scouts." Brad pulled his toque over his ears.

"Well, I still come once in a while for old time's sake."

Brad collapsed beside Kenny and Tommy Ho. They poked him and snickered. "You can sit with your girlfriend if you like," Tommy said.

"Don't be silly." Brad heaved a sigh of relief. He was glad to be here. He'd done his collecting, gotten the rest of his money from customers, and fifteen dollars in Christmas tips, including the one from Mrs. Chan, the Buddhist. He was curious about Buddhism. Maybe he needed a little Zen in his life. He pulled his mind back to the present, to the smell of wet mitts, the sound of laughter and chatter, the crunch of hay and frosty breath of horses. Now it was his turn, his turn to have fun. Relax like Mr. Traynor said.

"Where's Lane?" he asked.

Kenny pointed. Lane Traynor was in deep conversation with Matt, Junk and Junk's older sister. Brad waved at her. She'd seen him but she turned away.

The older Traynors and Mr. Bates were bundled up sitting on a bench across the front, keeping an eye on the rowdy crowd. Brad went up just before the wagon took off. He walked by Lane and Matt Peebles. "Great night for a party," he said.

"Don't tell me Einstein has decided to rejoin the human race," Lane sneered.

Brad shook his head as if he had been punched on the jaw. What had he done to deserve that? It hadn't sounded like Lane at all.

"Do you like the new car?" Anna Traynor smiled. "Grant wanted to buy a motorcycle but it's not practical for winter."

"The car's terrific." Brad stared at Lane. Why was Lane giving him the cold shoulder?

"Giddyup!" The wagon lurched as the driver called to the horses. Kenny pulled Brad down beside him.

The wagon headed for the woods. Someone started to sing:

Oh, you can't get to heaven on a Yonge Street car
'Cause a Yonge Street car can't go that far.
Oh, you can't get to heaven wrapped in cellophane
'Cause you got to go the way you came.

The kids laughed. The song went on. Something about that song bothered Brad. "Oh, you can't get to heaven ... you got to go the way you came ..." He searched his memory for more clues, but a fog blocked him. Something about that group of boys and his father singing. Not around the piano though—in the memory they are outside in a pool or a hot tub. And he, Bradley, is smaller, not part of it, never part of it.

"The star of Bethlehem might have been an exploding sun," Brad said. "An old star dying. It collapses into itself and the light is so bright that you can even see it in the daytime." Brad warmed to his subject, safe on the firm ground of newly learned facts.

"Up to your old tricks, Bradley the brain," a voice shouted in the dark, one of his friends making fun of him. He moved to the back of the wagon and sat on the edge swinging his legs, watching the patterns the wheels made in the snow, the dips the horses' hooves made, the fresh pile of manure steaming on the track, the sharp smell of horse pee.

A couple of kids jostled and fought beside him. Azim and someone. Azim fell out, picked himself up and trotted after the wagon.

Suddenly Brad felt several hands on his back and elbows. He was pushed off, a flood of giggles following him as he rolled in the snow.

"It's not so easy climbing back on, brain," a voice said. "Think about it."

Azim had already pulled himself onto the wagon. Brad

brushed his snow-caked ski pants and trotted after the hay wagon. The breath in front of his face was thick. Clouds of exhaled breath, ice fog, circled the wagon. The Big Dipper hung straight up and down above them in the blue velvet sky.

Suddenly he slipped on a patch of ice and fell. By the time he pulled himself up, the wagon was several meters away from him.

Bradley ran then, tired, tripping, trying to catch up to the wagon. Lane, Ashley and Kenny were leaning on the tailgate. As he struggled to get onto the wagon, their hands, instead of reaching to help him, pushed him away.

"What's the matter with you guys?"

"Why don't you guess?" It was Lane's voice. Brad didn't know what to do. He was torn. Should he let the whole gang slide away or try to get them to change their mind. They were playing some silly children's game.

"Help me!" He stretched out his arms. His breath felt like it was tearing a hole in his chest. His feet slipped on the icy surface of the road. The darkness within met with the darkness outside and neither were friendly. "Please." Tears or sweat stung his eyes.

"We'll help you back on," Lane said. "But you've got to make a promise."

"What?" Brad whispered. He didn't have much stamina left. He could end up walking home from here.

"You've got to promise not to drop all your friends and disappear again," Lane shouted.

"It's not nice," Ashley said.

"I've been right here." Brad reached out his hand to Kenny. Kenny looked at Lane and then back at Brad.

"You've got to promise." Kenny grabbed Brad's hand, pulling him along.

Brad's chest was heaving. He gasped for breath, his lungs icy like they'd snap.

"I promise, I promise."

Arms reached down and yanked him back on.

"What's the commotion?" Mr. Traynor cried.

"Nothing, Dad," Lane answered. "Brad fell off the wagon, that's all. He's back on."

"Are you going to stay?" Kenny asked.

"I'm dreaming of a White Christmas," Mrs. Traynor started singing. The other adults joined in. The kids booed.

"Rudolph the red-nosed reindeer, had a very shiny nose," Ashley Sargent sang. Everyone sang along "... they wouldn't let poor Rudolf, join in any reindeer games."

"Brad," Lane sat with her mittened hands wrapped around her knees. "Someone had to teach you a lesson. When you disappeared into yourself like that we felt left out, like you didn't like us anymore. It hurt."

Brad pulled his gloves higher up on his wrists. He puckered his lips, squared his jaw. He'd never thought about that, but it made sense, the same way his memory self felt shut out by his dad and the big boys. He'd never thought about how his friends would feel.

Maybe growing up was like building a telescope. You choose the kind you want, but you need clear instructions, time and mega patience. Then you work. He'd just had a good dose of instruction, Lane-and-Kenny style.

"I hope the other instructions aren't so rough."

"What did you say?" Kenny asked.

"Nothing." Brad laughed and tossed a wad of snow from his pocket at his friend's face. "Nothing."

13. SHADOWS

BRAD COULD HEAR his father playing a medley of Christmas and New Year's pieces as he walked from the Traynors' car to the house. The notes rose in the crisp night air like flute song. The prairie sky was packed with millions upon millions of stars, the Milky Way turned sideways so he could see traces of the galaxies beyond. This view was accompanied by chords, melodies and rhythms from Desmond's fingers. For a moment Brad was caught feeling as if the music and the majesty of the sky weaved together to herald a new day, a day without panic or clouds, a day when he didn't feel as if he had done something wrong, forgotten something critical. Was that what Christmas and New Year's offered?

Brad slipped in the back door and tiptoed upstairs, checked that no one had broken the seal to his room: the transparent thread still stretched from the knob to the latch. He didn't want his parents seeing their gifts before it was time. He had broken his own rule, and allowed a plant in his room, a rare plant he'd bought for his mother at the conservatory in the city when the Scout troop had visited the planetarium, the museum and the conservatory one Saturday in November. He'd gone to the megamall, too, and bought his dad a tape recorder and microphone so he could record his own playing and singing. He'd love that.

Brad stretched out on the bed with his clothes on, listening to variations on "Winter Wonderland." He could listen to his father's playing for a long time, and forget the raised voice, the cynical remarks. Desmond played light classics, piano concertos with trills and haunting melodies. No heavy, brooding suites or largos. The darkness, the nervousness were saved for his eyes and his speech.

"*A beautiful sight, we're happy tonight, walking in a winter wonderland.*" His dad sang along with the piano.

His mom came home the day before Christmas, her face gray and drawn, her hands shifting newspapers, moving furniture, watering and trimming her plants. She and Brad put up the plastic tree and ornaments.

His father seemed relieved. In between trips to the city to play at the new hotel he talked about his work. He'd been noticed at the small piano bar in the suburbs and been hired by the El Rancho downtown. He was thrilled.

"The manager is so pleased with the customer response, he's added two more sets a night, at much better wages than that little dive I was in."

"That was a nice place, Des."

"But Una, this is so much better. New Year's Eve I'm featured in the restaurant and lounge, 'Des Gray, with the magic touch.'"

"Des Gray?" Brad asked. "Who's Des Gray?"

"That's my stage name, easy to say."

"What's the matter with our name?"

"When I told them my name was Desmond Greaves—rhymes with Leaves—they said it looked too much like Graves and the show would die like an old woman." He laughed.

"Oh, Desmond," Brad's mom sobbed.

"Sorry, Una, I forgot."

Brad shook his head. His dad could be pretty insensitive. His mom looked as if a strong breeze would blow her over.

☆

Christmas day was quiet. Brad's mom made cinnamon buns and Brad made scrambled eggs and bacon. They ate at the kitchen table. Then the three of them went into the living room and opened their presents.

Brad opened the envelope from his parents. "Thanks," he said. The cheque was for two hundred dollars. That was pretty generous. It would help pay for the rest of the equipment he needed for his telescope. He had asked for money. But maybe the little kid in him was a bit disappointed. What was he expecting?

Meanwhile his dad was carefully unwrapping his gift from Brad. He folded the Christmas wrapping paper and gave the bow to Brad's mom to save.

"I can make a real tape of my best renditions," his dad said. "Maybe even talk some recording company into putting out a CD of Des Gray." He hurried off to the music room.

Brad shook his head and turned to watch his mom's response to her present. She grinned and blushed. "Imagine, you buying a plant, Bradley. I know you don't like them much. Very thoughtful. Yes, indeed. Listen to that, Brad, your dad really loves his gift."

Desmond was playing songs over and over. Then the tape

would echo the melody. Brad shook his head. What a strange man. He obviously liked his present. But couldn't he have said something to Brad?

Brad's mom cleared a space in the dining room window for the rare plant with its leaves that closed when you put your fingers near them. It shrunk away from touch like his mom. That's why Brad had bought it for her. He knew she liked the plant, though. She kept strolling over and putting her fingers close to the leaves, smiling slightly as they flattened.

He sat holding the cheque. The mirror and eyepiece for his telescope were on order and should arrive in the next month or so. He was feeling pretty confident about getting the telescope finished by April. He had fifteen or so other projects underway that would guarantee that he won first prize at the Spring Science Fair. He wanted to get his picture in the city newspaper, big and bold on the cover of the Life Section, right where his dad would see it.

In the afternoon Kenny came over and they went to the rink and skated around, got into a pick-up game of hockey. Brad concentrated on enjoying himself, concentrated on the fact that this was a game. It worked. He had a good time.

"Why don't you come over to the house?" Kenny asked.

"I've got to get home and help with dinner," Brad lied. He didn't want to go over to the bustling Traynor house. He could just imagine all the laughter, lights, spilled games and puzzles. The cat would be tumbling in discarded wrapping paper and the dog would be begging for treats. The thought of it made him feel awkward.

When he got home, his mom had dinner on the dining room table. She had bought a paper table cloth with poinsettia and candles on it. A giant pointsettia sat in the middle. She was wearing a rose-colored sweater and she had put on lipstick. Even if she was in mourning, she was making a real effort. So would he. Brad raced upstairs and threw on his dress-up clothes; he wore them to church when he and his mother went.

His dad sat at the head of the table, dressed in his blazer and flannels. He blessed the food, then carved the chicken deftly. They ate in silence for a few minutes.

"They've got a big picture of me in the hotel lobby." Brad's dad helped himself to more stuffing. "They had a big city photographer take it and blow it up."

Brad's mom frowned. "I don't know whether that's a good idea …"

"Oh, for crying out loud, Una May, relax. Who's to know?"

"Desmond, I just worry …"

"You've been home, haven't you? You've been stewing over the past." He rose in his place, waving the carving knife like a weapon. His arms were taut as piano wires, his fists clenched. Desmond's new moustache curled, his fine black hair, darker than ever—was his father dying his hair?—fell in his eyes. His thin nose quivered in rage. "I shouldn't have let you go."

"Go clean your room, Brad." His mother backed away from his father towards the window. "I didn't talk to anyone, Des, I just cleaned the house out. Went to the church."

"Your mother said, go and clean your room."

"It's not dirty. We just started eating Christmas dinner."

"Don't raise your voice to me, young man. Una, he's your son." The poinsettia in the middle of the table waved in the breeze from all the movement. The three of them grouped by the dining room window in a triangle. Una May was trapped beside her new plant, its leaves all flat to the stem.

"Please, Brad," she pleaded.

Brad backed towards the hallway. He hated being shut out. He hated it so much that moment that something snapped inside him. His blood roared, his shoulders tightened. "I'm not a little kid any more. I want to know what is going on. I want to know what happened in Killop. What happened in Saskatoon? What are you hiding?"

Desmond's face flamed. Una's mouth quivered.

"Send him to his room, Mother." Dad's voice sounded old and flat. "He nearly killed you being born. Now he wants to break your heart." Desmond paced the floor, the worn carpet sucking up the sound of his feet. "Your mother and I have built a life of our own. We've built a life. You have no right, no right at all to question us—to interrogate us—you have no right." He paused. "It's nobody's business. Nobody's. If you don't like it, feel free to leave." He marched to his studio. The door slammed.

Una's hands clenched the back of the chair. Brad stood as if struck by a punching bag, weaving back and forth, teetering on his broad feet.

"Sorry." He turned his head away.

"Des doesn't mean what he says. He's upset," his mother whispered. "He doesn't like living alone."

"I was here," Brad said under his breath. "I was here all the time, Mom."

His left foot was on the bottom step when his mother began talking quickly. "You came breach birth. Upside down. I was in labour all day." Her voice ran on. "Said I was too old, too old for complications. Could have killed me. Shouldn't have gotten pregnant. But I wanted a family so much, before it was too late. Risky, they said, risky business. And your father didn't want the bother, didn't come in the room with me. He hated the noise, the confusion, the blood. He wanted me home in a hurry. He hated living alone." Brad leaned on the banister, listening to his story, wishing he had been more gentle, an easier birth. He hadn't wanted to hurt her, ever. He ran his fingers over itchy eyes. "He never touched you, Brad. He thought babies were too messy. I didn't know it was going to be like that. I didn't know …"

His mother's face was twitching, the mouth on the frozen side jerking. She had been hurt enough, this woman. One of the difficulties of growing up was the whole business of living with each other. Everyone was so different. He didn't want to hurt other people. He'd just hurt his friends by trying to live alone as if he wasn't in a classroom, in a school, a Scout troop. Geez, how do you do it? He knew one thing for sure. He wasn't going to hurt his mother ever again. He vowed he would not add any more hurts and crossed his fingers as he thought it, to make it come true.

"Please, Brad, no more questions," she said. "Some things you're best not knowing. Believe me, I know more than I want to know. Ignorance may not be bliss, but it beats knowing as much as I do." She patted her hair, wandered into the kitchen and put on the kettle. Her compact body, in a too-short pink flowered skirt and her rose sweater, with sensible shoes and stockings, seemed insulated from the shocks the world delivered. Only her shaking hands, as she wiped the counters, wrung the dish rag and hung it over the towel bar, betrayed her.

Brad left her alone.

In the flurry of the last few minutes the card from his mother's plant had fluttered to the floor like a shedding leaf. Brad bent to replace it.

"From your loving son, Bradley," it said. Giving love

seemed so simple. All the birthday cards made it sound easy. But it wasn't. No wonder science and the stars attracted him. They did not hurt each other. Giving life, like his mother had given him, shouldn't have hurt so much. Did the Orion Nebula feel pain when a star was born?

14. NEW YEAR'S EVE

☆

BRAD FINISHED TWO more laps of the hotel pool before sinking in the hot tub to his neck. The heat brought pins and needles to his feet. It was New Year's Eve and his dad had gotten a room at the El Rancho for the night. A burly father and his two kids lolled around in the steam. The mother had disappeared into the sauna. The two kids laughed as Brad yelped from the heat.

"Pretty hot stuff," the girl said. She had long blond hair plastered to her head, braces and a narrow face.

"Hotter than yesterday." The boy used his hand as a jet squirting water at his sister. He had a shock of black hair standing on end in the steam and eyebrows so bushy you could lose a bird in them.

"Tell Jeffrey to stop, Dad."

"We're from Dallas, Texas," the boy addressed Brad, "visiting our grandparents for New Year's. It's sure cold here in winter."

Brad nodded. The guy stared at him.

"I live an hour outside the city," Brad said. "In Camden. It's a little place."

"On a farm?"

"Nope."

"I've never met a farmer."

"I'm not a farmer."

"Did you say farming?" The girl slid over beside him. Her bikini strap kept sliding off her left shoulder. "Do you ride tractors and hay balers?"

"No, a bike."

"I'm in oil," the father announced. "These kids have lived in cities around the world. Real globe-trotters."

The three of them studied Brad like he was a specimen in the zoo. He rubbed the back of his neck, feeling very self conscious. But he'd decided to give people a chance, pretend he was like Lane.

"We've moved, too," he said. "My dad's a musician." A fleeting image of his dad arose in the corner of his mind, his father in a hot tub in a back yard with a gang of big boys. His dad must have rented a hot tub for one of his student parties. Something about this memory made him feel uneasy, as if he had been a bad boy and couldn't remember how. He started to pull out of the tub. But the girl was talking to him, bending toward him.

"A musician. Oh, wow, like neat, guitars, big bands, country?"

The girl leaned so close strands of her blond hair fell on Brad's shoulder. "Maybe we know him."

"Not big time. He was nearly a concert pianist."

"Do you play? Jeffrey does, don't you, Jeffrey? I quit because practicing was a bore."

"Where's your dad performing?" their dad asked.

Brad gulped. "Here, in the hotel. He's in the restaurant and lounge."

"We heard him last night. He's good." Jeffrey swam over

and splashed Brad as he pulled up on the edge of the hot tub, his knee nearly in Brad's chin. Brad moved away. Give a guy some room, he said to himself.

"He's pretty good for an old guy." Jessica giggled. "I mean his music was old."

"Watch your mouth, Jessica." Her brother paused. "Don't mind her, my sister's a motor-mouth."

"Did they give you a hotel room free?" Jessica asked. "And your food?"

Brad shook his head. "I don't know."

Brad perched on the side of the tub beside Jeffrey, dangling his feet. The mother returned, tanned, blonde and beaded with perspiration. She stepped gingerly into the water, rescuing the curls at the nape of her neck from the steaming water.

"His dad is the guy playing the piano bar."

She smiled at Brad. "The one that made such a fuss over Jeffrey." Her husband chuckled.

"I have to get ready for tonight." Brad grabbed his towel and wrapped it around him. "More than ten minutes at a time in a hot tub and the human body is under a lot of stress."

"Catch you later," the boy hollered after him.

"What's your name—Des Gray, Junior, the farmer?" the girl shouted.

He took a step towards them. "Brad, Bradley Greaves, rhymes with leaves."

"Don't you use your dad's name?"

"He doesn't use our name. He uses a stage name." Brad turned his head away. He wanted the girl to stop asking questions, sitting there in the hot tub, interrogating him. He cracked his knuckles, moved to the elevator.

"Do piano men make good money?" she asked.

Brad gave up waiting for the elevator and took the stairs two at a time. Jessica was still talking as he flew up the steps. "Does he dye his hair? Wear a wig?"

What a motor-mouth.

☆

Brad and his mom and dad sat eating supper in the rotating restaurant, the shiny white piano idle at the far end of the room with tall glass panels, and the bar beyond. Purple stage lights gave the piano a lilac glow, a galaxy of twinkling lights bobbed in air currents above the stage.

"Quite a place, quite a place." Brad's mom pushed baby carrots onto her fork.

"We'll have a full house tonight," Desmond smiled. "A mittful of requests. The manager said he's never had anyone as good as me at playing what the customers request. It may not be Carnegie Hall but the tips are great. The tips are great."

Brad ate linguine.

"Don't inhale your food, Brad," his mother admonished.

His father reached across the table and grabbed Una's hand. "Is my tie straight, mother? Do you think my suit looks too shiny in the floodlights?" He smoothed his glossy black hair back from his forehead. It waved gently, wavier, darker than ever. The sporty new moustache gave him a less spooky look, his eyes seemed less haunted. "Too bad the old man never lived to see me. He'd be sorry. He'd be sorry," he muttered.

Una May leaned across the table and adjusted the tie a trifle, turned down his collar. "He wouldn't have sold your piano."

Grandpa Greaves had sold Dad's piano. When? When he was a kid? Brad sat, his fork empty in his hand.

His father leaped to his feet, tugging his trousers down. "Here come my fans."

Jessica and her family settled between the piano and the dance floor. Desmond made his way to the piano to a smattering of applause. The Texans clapped loudly. Jeffrey moved to one of the high stools beside the piano.

The waitress brought Brad a gooey slice of mud pie. Chocolate syrup covered the plate. His mother asked for more coffee.

Jessica, wearing a sparkly blue dress that made her look older, headed across the floor to their table.

"I thought you might come over and see me, Bradley Greaves, rhymes with leaves." She turned to Brad's mom. "Hi, Brad and I met in the pool this afternoon."

"The hot tub," Brad corrected her.

"Aren't you going to introduce me to your grandmother?"

"This is my mom. Mom, this is Jessica." Brad glared at her.

"Oh, sorry. The lights in here make everyone look real old."

Brad laughed. He'd have to get this girl away. Every time she opened her mouth she put her foot in it.

"I'll come over to your table as soon as I've slurped this mud pie," he said.

Jessica shrugged, "Oh, hey, like I didn't mean you were old or anything, I thought maybe you'd all like to join us, but then you seem so reserved." She left.

"Nice girl, Brad."

"She's a motor-mouth. You don't look that old, not in that rose dress." Brad blushed. His mother smiled a crooked smile that warmed him through and through. His dad played the medley Brad had heard him practicing when he came home from the hay ride.

"Why did Grandpa Greaves sell Dad's piano?"

"They needed the money. I don't know." She twisted her wedding ring, fumbled with her napkin. "Your father never forgave him. I often wish he'd fought it out with the old man, stood up to him. But that was long before I knew him, long before he came to Killop, long before you were born. Let sleeping dogs lie, Bradley. I don't know what's gotten into you lately, wanting to know so much."

Brad watched his mother fold and refold her napkin, move the silverware, straighten the salt and pepper shaker. *I want to know who I am*, he screamed in his head, *I want to know where I came from. What's so wrong with that?*

The audience applauded as Mr. Greaves finished the set. He came over to the table accompanied by a heavyset man in a black tuxedo.

'This is the hotel manager." Desmond's voice was flattering, sweet. "I want him to meet my little family. My dear wife, Una May, and my son, Bradley. He's the baby of the family, big for his age."

"Welcome to El Rancho." The man's hand shaking Brad's was sweaty and smelled of harsh soap. "Des here is a great addition to the El Rancho family, to our entertainment. Glad you could join him."

"Pleased, I'm sure," Brad's mom bobbed her head a couple of times like a duck swallowing crumbs.

"When you live in the city, we'll see more of you, I'm sure." He looked at Brad. "Your father tells me you're quite the scientist, an inventor, too."

Brad blushed to the roots of his hair. His father came silently behind him, patted him on the shoulder. "A chip off the old block. If I hadn't been so talented, I would have been a scientist. I had the grades for it, best in the west."

"Keep up the good work, boy." The florid man checked

the fake hankie in his pocket. "Nice meeting you folks. Have to visit the ballroom, the dinner theatre and the pub before midnight. Ta-ta. Don't get dizzy, staring out the window at the city as it orbits."

Through the tinted glass the lights of New Year's flashed and sparkled. Reds and greens outlined condo balconies, miniature white bulbs filled the trees on the legislature grounds, flashing blue lights swung in the wind on the arm of a massive crane over a new high rise.

Brad stood politely as the man left. Jessica waved, patting the seat beside her.

"Did I tell you I saw the Traynors wandering around downtown earlier this evening celebrating First Night? I told them to join us for midnight," Brad's dad grinned. "Kenny wants to hear me play."

"Excuse me," Brad said. He had to get away from his folks.

"Where's he going, mother?"

Brad threaded his way across the crowded restaurant. About one hundred seats with fifteen left vacant. The room revolved once every ninety minutes, the waiter had said. His father had talked about him to the manager. His father was thinking of moving to the city. Why did life keep happening in waves like the sea, up one minute, down the next? A guy could get dizzy.

"You took long enough to get here," Jessica giggled. "Grandpa, Grandma, this is Bradley, the farmer."

"I'm not a farmer."

"Oh, right. I forgot. Brad's the pianist's son, the guy Jeffrey envies."

"Imagine listening to him play every day." Jeffrey nursed a tall glass of chocolate milk. His black hair drooped into his steely blue eyes.

"Your dad's very talented," the father repeated. "He needs an agent. They'd love him in Dallas. I wonder if I know someone."

"It's New Year's Eve, Harry. You promised, no business," his wife teased.

"Brad isn't like his daddy, are you Brad?" Jessica chuckled. "He's a country boy. There, I didn't call you a farmer. You must have some hidden talent."

Brad shook his head, 'no'.

The rotating restaurant had them facing the river valley where there were fewer lights. Brad decided to take the offensive. "If you look out the window you will see Orion the Hunter and all the other stars of the winter sky."

"Oh ho, the sleeping giant awakes," Jessica commented.

"We're sitting in this restaurant as it rotates once every ninety minutes." He could feel his ears getting hot, but he pressed on. "Meanwhile the Earth is rotating once a day, which means we are actually travelling 1,350 kilometers an hour. And the Earth is moving around the sun, so we are really travelling 45,000 kilometers per hour. All of us are in some orbit or another."

"Like who are you?" Jeffrey raised his bushy eyebrows two notches. "Einstein?"

"I'm impressed," Jessica said. "I want to be a scientist when I grow up, an earth scientist."

"You do?" Brad was surprised.

"Hey, Brad, Happy New Year! Buffalo biscuits, Lane, he's found a girlfriend." Kenny bounced across the room and stood beside Brad. Lane came more slowly. She was dressed better than Brad had ever seen her, a dress made of layers and layers of flimsy plum material. Lane was trying to walk sedately in slippers instead of sneakers. Brad grinned. She looked as self-conscious as he felt. She grinned back.

"Look who's wearing a suit." Kenny tugged at Brad's sleeve. The three buddies snickered at the joke. Jeans and t-shirts were more their style.

"It's only for one night," Brad laughed.

His father started playing again. The Texans, the Traynors, Brad and his mom gathered around three tables close to the piano. Brad ordered nachos. Jessica ordered veggies and dip. The waiter brought soft drinks for them.

As midnight approached the crowd in the restaurant became noisier and noisier. Mrs. Traynor and Brad's mom talked. The Texans and the American kids' grandparents danced. Jessica, Lane and Brad played a video dart game.

Jeffrey and Kenny sat on stools close to Desmond.

"Countdown," Desmond called into the microphone. "Ten, nine, eight, seven ..."

Everyone joined in. "Six, five, four, three, two ..."

"One! Happy New Year's, everybody!" Desmond played a massive chord. People picked up whistles, horns and squeakers and the room became a slowly whirling circus of hats, kisses, hugs and music.

Grant and Anna Traynor hugged and kissed, then grabbed their kids. Jessica circled the crowd kissing everyone, including Brad, who looked startled. Brad pecked his mother's cheek. His father sat playing, alone on his stage.

The crowd made a circle of hands and arms.

"Should auld acquaintance be forgot ..." Brad's mother broke away from the group and went over to Desmond, put her hand on his arm, nodded, then sat on the stool closest to him.

"Blue moon," Desmond played and sang, *"I saw you standing alone, without a dream in your heart, without a love of your own."*

"They're pretty old," Jessica reflected, "but they still need company."

"All of us need someone," Lane said.

"Maybe," Brad muttered. "Do I get to choose who?"

Shortly after midnight the hotel photographer came around taking promotional shots.

"Here," Brad's dad cried gleefully. "I want a group shot." Brad and his mom moved toward the piano, expectantly.

"Kenny, Jeffrey, come here. The three musicians—beats the three musketeers." Desmond's voice echoed across the room.

Disappointment registered on Brad's mother's face. Brad turned his head away.

Desmond wrapped an arm around each boy and pulled them close so their heads rested one on his right and the other on his left shoulder. The boys' faces were flushed, their eyes feverish. Kenny looked at the crowd, an expression of happiness mixed with something else.

Brad's mother reached out a shaky hand as if to pluck a dying leaf from a plant.

A slice of cold ran down Brad's back and he stared out the window at the moving sky. He would win the prize, he would have his picture taken, receiving the reward and his mother would be there. His father played again. The chords jarred in Brad's head and the melody was lost in the din.

A dense fog gathered in the river valley as the restaurant rotated into the night.

15. A GOOD DEED

*Found this quote while I was reading. Thought you might
like it, seeing as you like the planets so much.*

                                        J. Drum

p.s. Here's ten dollars for the last three weeks of the
Journal. *Keep the change.*

"*The fair humanities of the old religion ... live no longer
in the faith of reason. But still the heart doth need a language; still doth the old instinct bring back the old names;
spirits or gods that used to share this earth with man as
with their friend; and at this day 'tis Jupiter who brings
whate'er is great and Venus who brings everything that's
fair.*" — *Coleridge*

BRAD TOOK THE typed quote, folded it, and put it in his
wallet. He debated about wearing gloves, decided against it,
sprinted down the stairs to his bike.

The first Saturday in April had dawned bright and clear.
A few dingy snowbanks clustered along the roadways, by
sidewalks, forlorn remnants of once brave white peaks. Giant puddles and rivers of muddy water, coated with a thin

layer of black ice, crackled in the morning sunlight.

Brad wheeled through each puddle with a broadening smile as his tires pierced the ice and the twin tracks appeared behind him. No wonder little kids slop around in ditches and potholes where goo and gumbo collect. The sounds of breaking ice, sloshing water, and the smell of oil and mud released when he and his bike broke through the sheets of frozen muck filled Brad with a feeling of power. He breathed deeply.

Sun shone on his bare head, his toes in worn sneakers were wet and cold from water splash and ground chill. Brad heard the whisper of his breath, felt the flowing of his blood beneath the skin, the pulling of the muscles in his calves. *Too bad I have to grow up and leave this perfect feeling, too bad old guys can't have fun like this. Take Dad, he's so busy stewing over money, griping at Mom and me because we don't want to move to the city, boasting about his latest fans.*

Up ahead something banged, then banged again. Not sharp like gunfire, nor soft like a closing door, but hollow-sounding like someone hitting a culvert.

Old Drum and his dog stood in front of the old man's house. Drum was chopping ice from the driveway near the storm sewer. The Irish setter, with dirty paws and mud-flaked flanks, sat watching, eyes blinking with each strike of the hoe.

The old man stopped and leaned on his hoe, sighing as the giant puddle began to drain away, gurgling and gushing into the freed drain.

"Hi, Mr. Drum, thanks for the poem." Bradley grinned and splashed through the rushing river to the curb, put his sodden sneaker down on the squishy brown grass. "Working hard?"

The dog trotted over and sniffed Brad's damp pant leg. Old Drum smiled, his wrinkled face flushed and shiny, a battered gray fedora perched on his head wet with sweat.

"No way! I was itching to get outside and do something useful. Time I rejoined the human race. I'm just hurrying on the spring," Drum chuckled. "Hear you're goin' over to clean up Sawdust Johnny's. Now that's hard work." The old man wiped rough hands on green overalls and went back to banging ice.

"The Scout troop is doing it," Brad mounted his bike "... and some of the moms and dads."

The old man was talking so low Bradley rode closer to hear. "I went to school with Sawdust Johnny, seems like a century ago. He was just plain Johnny Smith back then, hadn't made a name for himself, hadn't wheeled barrows full of sawdust home to put in his woodstove. He was just a dumb kid, really slow, you know. He couldn't learn anything. Couldn't sit still, couldn't learn his numbers. Teacher put a desk at the back of the room. He came to school pale, sometimes bruised and always smelled of pee. Social Services tried to get him taken from the family ... but they couldn't. Not back then. Wouldn't happen in Camden nowadays. There's laws against abusing kids."

"We'll clean up his house, fill the cupboards, wash his clothes." Brad tasted metal on his tongue. His stomach churned.

"Good deeds, eh, my boy? Taking care of the crippled, the poor, the old, that's working for the community. It's danged important." Old Drum set the hoe against the elm. "Worry about Sawdust Johnny's eyes these days. They look far away as if he's left us completely. Not that the world would miss the old bugger ..." Drum reached in his pocket, pulled out a huge white hankie, fished deeper and brought out a five-dollar bill.

"Buy him some sweet and sour candies. When I brought

a bag to class, he made a funny sucking noise with them." Old Drum sighed. "In some ways he's still a kid, never grew up and took care of himself. If he asks, tell him Juno Drum sent them. He'll remember me. I was the biggest boy in the school, big for my age, same as you, Brad Greaves. Big boys need lots of room. It's hard being big, people think you're all grown up. But you aren't. Not by a long shot. Hell, I'm still learning."

Brad stuffed the money in his pocket and rode away. He couldn't imagine Old Drum as a big boy. He must have shrunk. Drum's setter loped along beside Brad in the spray from the puddles, then peeled off to do his morning orbit of the town.

Brad pulled into the middle of the silent morning street and pumped pedals, whistling through his teeth, thinking about old men and boys and candies and puddles and chopping ice and how sad life was one minute and happy the next.

Buckles had been there. His share of the papers was gone and the straps and scraps lay in a heap by the side of Brad's bundle. At least Buckles never bothered the papers any more, not since Brad threatened him. Every time they saw each other at school Buckles' eyes looked daggers, his shoulders tightened, and he whispered to his greasy friends.

Brad shrugged, tossed the garbage in the oil drum at the corner and pedaled away to deliver his papers.

At home Brad changed into dry jeans, an old sweat shirt and hiking boots. His father was practising piano. His mom scrambled eggs.

"Where is it you're going, dear?" She put a plate of eggs, bacon and toast in front of him.

Brad told her as he shoveled food into his mouth.

"Talking with your mouth full again, Bradley?" His father pulled out a chair and sat opposite, poured himself a glass of orange juice. Una brought his plate to the table.

Brad's toes curled in his sneakers, as if he were getting ready to run. He chewed his toast. The electric clock clicked as the minute hand passed the hour hand. The kettle whistled.

Brad picked up his empty plate, glass and cutlery and bent over the dishwasher. "Got to go," he mumbled.

"When I was his age, I worked in a grocery store," his father said. "Worked ten hours every Saturday bagging potatoes and delivering groceries. Didn't have time to run around playing games with Scouts."

"Bradley's got his paper route, Desmond," Una sighed.

The back of Brad's neck flushed, the cords in his throat stiffened. "We're not playing, we're helping clean up Sawdust Johnny's." He wanted to add, and most of the dads are coming, too, but the words stuck in his gullet.

"Waste of time, if you ask me. That dirty old man made it through the winter without your help, and he'll make it through the spring." Desmond was shouting. He rose in his place, waved his hands as if he were conducting a full orchestra. "If you clean up his cabin, he'll have it just as dirty in a week. Probably has lice. Don't bring home lice, Brad." His eyes, big at the best of time, were huge and glazed, his Adam's apple leapt up and down as he talked.

Brad's mother pushed cold eggs around her plate, raised her eyes, put down her fork. "It's a good thing to do, Des, it's a good thing."

Brad backed out of the room as his father spoke. "You know

very well, Mother, there are some people you just can't help."

Brad unlocked his bike and rolled away. The dead hedge scratched the back of his hand when he veered close to the carragana bushes in the laneway. He steered with his right hand and sucked the stinging scratches on the back of his other hand as he rode. His eyes felt scratchy too, and the back of his throat, but there was nothing he could do to fix them.

The Traynors' van was parked by the ravine, close to Sawdust Johnny's cabin. Brad threw his bike in the tall grass, shoved his hands in his pockets and strode over. Junk clung to the roof, cleaning out the eavestrough, and Bait held the bottom of the ladder. Mr. Bates and Grant came out of the house carrying a filthy overstuffed chair. Dust clouds billowed as they whacked it with brooms. Mr. Bates went back inside the shack.

Matt Peebles and his mom waved as they carted green garbage bags of clothes and linen to their car. "We'll put these in the laundromat and be right back."

Lane, Ashley and Kenny stood by a flaming oil drum, tossing rotten junk in it. All of them looked like they wished they had gas masks.

Sawdust Johnny sat on an upturned orange crate smoking a bent cigarette.

"Your dad coming, Brad?" Bait asked.

Brad shook his head, no. He kicked a can in the direction of the recycle box where Mrs. Traynor was running a hose over all the dishes and bottles.

"Why don't you bring out the books and newspapers,

Brad? We could bundle them."

Brad walked into the tar-papered shack. Mr. Bates washed the windows with one hand and held a hankie to his nose with the other. The smell hit Brad.

"Holy cow." His breakfast rose in his throat. He turned and ran from the cabin, tripped over a beer bottle in the grass and sprawled in the yard.

"We know it smells bad, Brad, but not that bad," Mrs. Traynor laughed. Brad flung his bangs from his eyes and turned to answer her. He saw red.

"It's not funny."

"Oh, Brad, lighten up." Ashley came around the side of the house. "You take everything too seriously."

Bait leaned against the ladder giggling. "You should see yourself, like funny or what?"

Brad picked himself up and ran a comb through his hair, sending a shower of straw every which way.

"You've just earned your humility badge," Junk roared from the top of the ladder and tossed a big clump of dead leaves, twigs and gross goop from the housetop.

Brad dodged it and trotted back into the house for the newspapers and books. His ears burned. He pinched his nostrils together and grabbed a pile of papers and lumbered out of the house, bowed under the weight, acting like it was twice as heavy as it was. Maybe if he acted the fool, Ashley would forget he'd been so dumb.

Soon everyone was giggling. Grant Traynor brought out the coffee thermos and the soft drinks and doughnuts. Matt and his mom pulled up just in time for break. Matt grabbed three crullers at once.

Sawdust Johnny took a doughnut in each hand and walked away. He hadn't been on his rounds yet. He had bottles to find, wood to rescue, sawdust to collect, important work to do. He left.

"Old Drum went to school with him," Brad held up the five-dollar bill. "Wants me to buy him sweet and sours."

Two motorcycles roared down the street heading for the country. Buckles rode on the back of one. He screamed above the motors.

"Bunch of goody-goody boys. Wimps." Then he made a rude hand gesture.

"And girls, too." Lane stuck her tongue out.

The whole troop laughed and went back to work.

16. THE FIRE

☆

"WON'T BE LONG until the Fair." Kenny fingered Brad's diorama of the solar system. Lane sat at Brad's computer playing the stargazer's quiz. The three of them were supposed to be planning a sports day for the Beavers, Brownies and Cubs.

"How many entries does this make, Bradwurst?" Lane asked. "Kenny's just finished a terrarium, butterfly collection and global spice chart."

"Fourteen entries so far," Kenny said.

"Seventeen," Brad said proudly. In his mind he could see the color photograph in the *Journal*, he and his mom, accepting the prize. "Brad Greaves, winner of the Camden Science Fair. Local boy places first with the most winning entries ever."

"Come and see the nifty mounting I made for my binoculars."

"What about your telescope?" Kenny asked.

"It's under wraps in the garage. I still have to install the mirror and eyepiece, a six-inch Dobsonian Reflector. Real powerful. Pivots on its own, and is portable so I can take it camping when I have a van. Putting it together tried my patience." He led them onto the balcony.

His father's voice drifted up from the yard where he was painting the fence.

"I've got a terrible headache, mother. I don't think I'll go to your little office party after all."

"You promised ..."

"The smoke, the crowds, it's not my style."

"Unless they're in a hotel bar applauding." Una May Greaves' words were sharp and high-pitched.

"I get tired driving back and forth. It's your fault, Una, insisting on staying here."

"I've got to work, Des, and Brad's in school." There was a mutter. "Who knows how long your job at the hotel will last."

"You think more of that child than you do of me. I married you."

"You won't let me forget that, will you?"

"You're the one who keeps bringing up the past," Brad's dad muttered. "Don't touch the brush, Una, you'll get paint all over your hands. That wouldn't do for the top saleswoman of Miller Real Estate. Go to your little celebration. I'll tidy up out here and then rest my eyes. Enjoy yourself." Desmond's cold voice sliced the evening air.

"Don't try blackmail, Desmond." Una Greaves' voice rose. "Don't try blackmail with me. I've got more ammunition than you do." The screen door banged as she went back into the house.

"Parents!" Brad blushed. "Let's go plan this Sports Day."

The three kids went back into Brad's room.

"You can't move away, Brad." Lane plopped down on his old chair. Kenny stretched out on the bed.

"Our folks don't bicker, they discuss," Kenny laughed. "Dad gets into trouble because he's too busy, forgets birthdays and doesn't put away his tools. Mom yells at us because she hates housework."

"We all hate housework. The dog and cat don't help."

"Planning on training them to do dishes?" Brad laughed. He sat at this desk.

"No, dork, I mean they make more mess. And speaking of a mess ... if we don't make plans, the Sports Day will be a mess."

"What do we need?" Brad asked.

"Prizes, volunteers, events ..." Lane answered.

"Slow down, will you." Kenny had pulled himself into an upright position. "Okay, Brad, you take notes."

Brad could hear his mother banging around in her room, drawers opening and closing, hangers in the closet shifting. He tried to block out the sounds.

"How long should we make the races—100 meters?"

Later, after the plans were made, Brad took Kenny and Lane back out onto the balcony to gaze at the stars. Lane ran a hand over the binoculars, bent to take a look.

"The Big Dipper is straight overhead." Brad put one hand on Lane's shoulder and pointed. "Follow the arc to Arcturus and speed on to Spica. The arc is the Dipper's handle. There's Leo the Lion, Castor and Pollox the twins—Gemini—and this year Jupiter is visible. By the week of Spring Fair Mars, Venus and Jupiter will all be in sight. That's rare."

Downstairs, Desmond began to play a piece by Chopin. The music sounded far away.

"You and your folks live on different planets," Kenny said.

"Kenny, shut up, gnat brain," Lane hissed.

"Snot-face," Kenny parried.

"It's okay," Brad whispered. Life wasn't like television sitcoms or sloppy movies. Families aren't perfect. He knew that. He'd known for some time that his mom and dad and he weren't much alike, and having Kenny say it out loud, having friends who understood and wanted to keep him company, made it easier somehow.

"I smell smoke," Lane hollered. She pushed past Brad to the railing and hung her head out.

"Be careful," Kenny called.

"Yes, mother."

A strange glow lit up the northern sky. The town fire alarm howled. Brad threw the cover over his fancy equatorial mounting and the binoculars. Kenny raced for his bike. Soon the three of them were barreling along the side street in the direction of the pillar of flames.

Mr. Greaves had followed them to the door, studied the billows of smoke and flames on the horizon and returned to his piano. As Brad pedaled around the corner he could hear strains of Stravinsky's *Fire Dance*. His father didn't really live in Camden. He lived in his music. A stab of pain sharper than a sliver of glass pierced Brad. In some ways his father was more distant than when he had been away in hospital all those times, suffering from nerves, having his breakdowns. Like Kenny said, he lived on a different planet.

Buckles drove by on a motorcycle with no muffler, clinging to the black dude Brad had seen at his house.

"You're too big, now, buddy, for that guy to beat up on you." Kenny wheeled towards the scrub lot where the fire burned. "He'd be a stupid fool."

"Bradley's so big, his head's in the clouds," Lane simpered.

"Cut it out, Lane. You sound like Ashley," Kenny joked. "Too precious for words."

"It's a phase she's going through," Lane said. "Mom says she'll grow out of it. Ashley spends hours putting on her face, shopping, and listening to music videos. All she talks about is boys and clothes."

"Sounds boring," Brad said. "Is that what teenage girls do?"

"Are you kidding?" Lane punched him. "I'd rather chase fire trucks."

"It's Sawdust Johnny's!" Brad shouted.

"Buffalo biscuits!"

"Did we leave paint rags or thinner?" Brad asked.

"What a blaze."

Two fire trucks and an ambulance, two police cars, their blue lights flashing, hoses spurting water full stream onto the dilapidated house and the field behind. Firefighters in yellow slickers, boots and some with masks. The main beam crackled and crashed. A sudden burst of smoke and flames broke through the roof.

"Stay back. Stay back there." The police had cordoned off the yard where this morning the Traynors' van had been parked.

Brad pushed through the crowd to the front. The bystanders shouted to each other.

"It's a write-off."

"They have to stop the sparks from reaching the trailer park."

"They're evacuating the residents."

"Is that so?"

"My aunt lives there."

"Ironic, Bradley, isn't it?" said a voice beside Brad's elbow, a faint whiff of after-shave and boot polish. Old Drum grasped his elbow.

"Sir?"

"You fixed the house this morning and it burned down tonight. That's irony."

"It might be our fault," Brad said. "We might have left paint rags or something. Mr. Traynor doesn't always remember everything."

"Looks like a chimney fire to me," Old Drum said. "Sawdust, more than likely."

"I bought the candies."

"Knew you would."

A commotion erupted on the trampled soggy grass in front of the house. Two attendants from the ambulance pushed through the crowd to the group on the lawn who had emerged from the side of the building. A stretcher was laid on the ground. A crowd of police, firefighters and ambulance attendants surrounded it. All Brad could see was one dirty calloused foot with hammertoes and blisters, and that foot kept falling off the stretcher. Someone tucked it under the stark white sheet. But Brad could not erase its memory from his mind. He wondered whether his mind had been branded with the sight of that lifeless limb. Was the mind a thin skin that could be seared with ugliness or pain? He watched the scene before him as if it were happening outside himself. Except it wasn't. His skin was clammy, his eyes smarted from the smoke and evil-smelling fumes. Someone in the crowd sobbed. The silent people responded to the cry. They came alive, chattering, pointing, blowing noses, lighting cigarettes. Life moved on. The wheeled base under the stretcher was raised and the group moved the body to the ambulance, the crowd parting like a wave flung back from a jagged rock. Sawdust Johnny was dead.

"Never could take care of himself." Mr. Drum rubbed smoke and sweat from his eyes. His face had a pasty cast, like uncooked dough. Brad moved closer to the old man, was tempted to shelter him from the charred and sodden pile of wood and shingles, the absurd sight of a toilet bowl leaning against a smashed TV.

"I hope he ate all the candies." The words sounded so silly but the boy could not think of anything else to say. Brad had left the sweet and sours in a cracked white cereal bowl. Lane and Mrs. Traynor had picked a bunch of early flowers, dewdrops, wild roses and ferns and put them in an empty pop bottle sitting on the scrubbed arborite table beside the goodies. The Scout group had whistled as they gathered the garbage and tools.

Sawdust Johnny had come back from his rounds and sat on the green chair with the stuffing coming out of the arms—rocking back and forth, back and forth—saying nothing, just nodding, sucking loudly on the candy in his toothless mouth.

"I forgot to tell him you sent them, Mr. Drum, I'm sorry." Brad blew his nose. "I thought I'd tell him later." There wasn't going to be any later. Brad watched as the ambulance inched its way through the puddles from the hoses. It was in no hurry. "It's absurd, completely absurd. Life. Death."

The night air turned chilly. The fire turned to smoke and foul fumes. People began to leave. Brad looked around for Lane and Kenny and could not spot them. He leaned heavily on his handlebars, suddenly tired to the bone as if he too were an old man.

"Cocoa, Bradley?" Old Drum asked.

Brad nodded. They walked, Brad with his bike on the curb side, Mr. Drum marching like a retired general.

"Not a pretty way to die. If there is a pretty way," Old Drum's voice was hoarse. "Maybe the fumes got him."

"We thought about cleaning the chimney." Brad was still poking at the day. "Grant said there wasn't time and we'd leave it for fall … We should have done it today."

"It's nearly summer. You didn't know he was going to build a sawdust fire hot enough to set the soot in the chimney ablaze." Drum moved down the street. "You aren't to blame."

"But we should have cleaned it."

"It's not your fault," Old Drum spoke firmly. "Sawdust Johnny's death is no one's fault."

"But … "

"Leave it, boy. It's called random evil. There is random good, too. A scientist like you should recognize that. Some phenomena are unpredictable. You are not to blame, no one is. Life is sweet and sour, like them candies, you have to take it all into yourself." The old man shook his head. "Pardon me, I'm running on like a brook. I've kept to myself too long. It's like Johnny's death opened up a whole mess of words and thoughts and wanting to talk. Do you mind?"

Brad shook his head 'no'. He understood. He'd tried shutting himself away with all those projects. It hadn't worked.

The two of them walked down the street talking. Brad told Mr. Drum about the Spring Fair, and his entries. Mr. Drum listened and nodded his head. He mentioned the almost fight between Brad and Buckles. "I saw the two of you. Didn't say anything at the time … Didn't know you well. Wasn't ready."

Mr. Drum made Brad feel like they'd known each other for years—like he, Bradley, wasn't a kid at all—like they were two old friends.

"I've been watching you," Old Drum said as they approached his house. "You're a good paper boy, one of the best I've had. You are dependable and you work hard. You have to work on your temper. Knowing when to use the anger and when to let it go—that's part of growing up. You're stronger than you think. You aren't used to being so big, just like I wasn't when I was your age. I decided this morning, when you stopped to listen to my jawing, that we might be friends. Being an old widower is not much fun. Most of my friends are dead or in nursing homes. Since Florence died, I've kept to myself. After tonight I don't think that's such a smart idea."

The moon rose. The Dipper pointed straight up. Brad's face was struck by moonlight.

"So you want to be an astronomer. I've seen you out there, night after night with your binoculars. It's either stubbornness, cussedness or drive."

"I like the stars." Brad licked his lips. The air tasted sweet and still and the fire was far away.

"When I was your age, I wanted to be a train engineer." Old Drum unlocked his door and led the way to the tiny kitchen with its clean white table and chairs. Drum put on the kettle. The old dog wandered up from the basement where he had been sleeping. He sat quivering with joy, his wand of a tail thumping the polished linoleum floor.

"All prairie boys listened to the whistle and the roar each night as the big trains rolled by, wondering where they were going, what they were carrying. Without the trains going through each day, it would have been hard to believe there was a world out there. I loved the rumble, the shiny engines, the wave from the driver."

The kettle whistled, startling them. Maybe they were expecting an old-fashioned train to roar through the kitchen instead of a just seeing a small pot of water boiling loudly on the stove.

Brad shivered. Old Drum spooned out the cocoa.

"I had the best model train outfit in town. I made all the scenery myself."

"Do you still have it?" Brad asked, delighted.

"Well, a modest collection." The old man grinned. "I grew up and chased my dream. I was an engineer for the CNR for thirty-five years before I came back here to retire with Florence, my wife."

They sat opposite each other stirring hot chocolate, sipping, slurping, and munching on store-bought vanilla sandwich cookies.

"I hope you don't mind keeping an old man company for an hour or so. Every time someone dies, even a poor old soul like Sawdust Johnny, I feel a little closer to death myself. Made me think I'd like to live a little longer, make some new friends, share their dreams."

Brad glanced into Old Drum's pale blue eyes; safe, steady, comforting eyes.

"I'd love to see your trains," he said.

"Would you, now? Well, it just so happens I've set them up in the basement, waiting for a good workout. You can choose which engine you want to drive."

The old dog woofed, wagged his tail and led the way.

17. BINGO

SNOW FELL IN great gobs from a totally gray sky, piling up on the grass, melting on the road and coating sidewalks and driveways, except where patches of oil lay. Hard to believe it was May, the week of the Spring Fair.

Brad walked down the aisle of the bingo hall. The room was filled with smoke and talk. People were buying cards from Dr. Peebles and Mr. Bates. Some had four or more cards in front of them, piles of the small green plastic discs or markers, cups of coffee, cigarettes. Lane and her mom were doing a roaring business in the concession. Brad and Tommy Ho were delivering drinks.

The loudspeaker crackled. "Testing, one, two, three." The caller cleared his throat. The rollers whirled. "Under the O ..."

"Hey, kid, give me a diet cola." A giant woman in a pink sweat suit who Brad had seen in the post office and on the main street, grabbed his elbow. "Be quick about it."

She had twelve cards spread in front of her, a cigarette burning in a half-filled ashtray. Her hands moved across the cards like fat minnows in a brook, darting, dropping discs on numbers faster than Brad could follow. He watched entranced.

"Give the kid the money, Rory," she ordered. Sitting beside her, hidden by her bulk, was Buckles. He sneered as he handed Brad the change. "Doing yur goody-goody deed for the day, Bradley?"

"Bingo!" A voice called from the far side of the hall. The fat woman scooped her discs up and raised her eyes. "Is this one of your friends from school, Rory?"

"He does papers, ma."

"What's your name, boy?"

"Brad, Brad Greaves,"

"You from here?"

"Brad's from Killop, same as us." Buckles said.

"What's your last name again, Graves?"

"No, Greaves, rhymes with leaves. My mom's from Killop, she's a Clark, Una May Clark."

"Una May Clark, woman with a big scar on her jaw, a frozen face? Used to sing in the United Church choir, taught me Sunday School. She your ma? I thought I seen her in Safeway a few months ago, figured it must be someone else. What a coincidence, you being friends with Rory and all."

Brad backed away, bumped into the guy at the next table. "Give me one of those sodas, boy."

"Under the I 16." The microphone cackled as the caller spoke.

Brad spent the next hour fetching and carrying. His feet hurt and his eyes stung from the smoke and the mixture of hot bodies, old perfume and clothes losing their freshness. Good thing the money would send a few of them to the Scout Jamboree.

A few minutes later Buckles' mom grabbed his elbow again. "Rory tells me you're something of a bully, picking on him."

Brad raised his eyebrows. Buckles was smirking like he had caught a fish and was frying it in hot oil.

"Must be in the blood." The woman shifted her weight. Oh, no. Here it comes. Brad braced himself.

"Seems yur folks left because of a scandal, Bradley the brain. Yur old man's weird. He was fired from the church, for God's sake." Buckles laughed loud like a hyena. "Wait till I tell the kids at school yur dad's an ex-con. He's been in prison, ya dork. Maybe he shared a cell with my old man, eh? Only my old man hasn't come back."

"Rory, shut up, don't go blabbing our business to the world." She lit a cigarette. "Poor Una May, marrying the church organist, the town's old maid with the broken face marrying the dapper musician. No one could see what they saw in each other. Then it came out."

"My dad's been in hospital. He has nervous breakdowns," Brad blurted.

"Under the N 24," the caller shouted.

"Nervous breakdown, that's a laugh. He's a sicko from jail. Wait until I tell the kids. They'll love it. The class brain, ya'll probably grow up just like your dad. Sick, all right, sick in the head. An old man who bothers kids, a pervert."

"Liar!" Brad reached for Rory's shoulders, gripped the kid in hands as tense as talons. He could feel anger boiling inside, bubbling through his chest and arms like a rampaging river. Bingo players gasped behind them.

"Someone haul this bully off my son," Mrs Buckles hollered. "Rory's right, you are dangerous."

As suddenly as he'd grabbed Buckles, Brad let go, his hands shaking. Colors danced in front of his eyes; blacks, reds, purples. It was as if his dream of falling from a space craft had come true. His sense of control slipped; he turned to face his enemy, the boy who always brought chaos with him, trailing behind him like a comet's trail of debris. Brad danced on the balls of his feet, daring Rory to hit him.

Rory's hands came up in a boxer's pose. His right fist connected with Brad's jaw.

Brad leapt on Buckles and knocked him to the ground, sat on him. He breathed rapidly, his heart pounded in his ears. He wanted to beat Buckles' face to a pulp, grind the smirk off his mouth, blacken the shifty eyes. Silence the voice that was ringing all the way to his toes. Pervert.

"That's enough," Mr. Traynor shouted. "That's enough!"

Brad looked up, dazed, to see his Scoutmaster, the crowd, the big woman in her pink jogging suit.

"Get off me, ya big oaf," Buckles laughed. "Next time, eh?"

"I don't like fighting," Brad said, exhausted suddenly, tired to the bone.

"So what do ya call this?" Buckles dusted off the seat of his pants. "Dancing?"

Brad shook his head to clear it, looked at Mr. Traynor, and took off his canvas apron.

"Where do you think you're going," Mrs. Buckholz hollered.

"Home." He handed Lane the money. Lane stared after him. Brad turned his face away. He could not look her in the eyes, felt too alien, too changed. He ran outside.

The cold night air exploded on his skin. The stars shone brilliantly. Brad threw his head back and let them comfort him, let the facts fall gently from the storehouse in his head, from the part of himself he could trust.

In our solar system there are ten planets with moons and rings. I live on one of those planets, in a familiar orbit where we can see thousands of galaxies, trillions of stars, white dwarfs, red dwarfs. I know about quasars, black holes, an expanding universe with new theories developing every week about more universes, more solar systems with invisible planets. My father is ... my father is ... one of those guys they warn you about in videos ... one of those bad-touch men. What does that make me?

Brad walked home to the darkened house. As he tiptoed past his mom's room he could hear her gentle snore. By his dad's room his body stiffened, his gut seized, his legs turned to jelly. So you wanted to know everything, Bradley, and didn't Dad say, didn't he say, what you don't know can't hurt you? That's what he said. I thought he was trying to protect me from finding out bad stuff about Mom's folks, bad things about Killop. It was bad news about him.

The light in his room hurt Brad's eyes. He would have preferred the dark. But he would trip over something if he left the light off. All his entries for the Spring Fair were boxed and tagged, the work of the last eight months ready to be taken to the Agricom tomorrow night: the diorama, telescope, video game, electrical inventions, card collection, star charts, and best of all the telescope in the corner.

Brad threw himself on the bed. The *Enterprise* model was packed so it wasn't swinging from the light fixture. To boldly go where no one has gone before. What a joke. He wasn't feeling brave and he didn't want to go, to school or to the Fair. Suddenly, none of it mattered. None of it mattered in the least. What did his dad do? He'd never touched Brad, never touched him at all. Not once.

He rolled onto the floor and pulled his knapsack and sleeping bag from the bottom of the closet. As he dug around in the dark his hand closed on something fuzzy and soft. Brad pulled it out. One of his old teddy-bear slippers—must have fallen out of the bag for the Goodwill—one of the tattered slippers that he had hung onto for years, even though he'd outgrown them long ago. He hadn't been able to part with them, not until last summer when Mom insisted that he stop acting like a pack rat. He held the slipper in his big hand and sheepishly leaned his cheek against it. It smelled of footsweat, mothballs and old houses. He should throw it out. He tossed it toward the wastebasket, but when it fell short he put it back in the closet. A faint whiff of kid smell lingered on his fingers, bringing a flood of unpleasant memories. A time when he had been bad, a dark time, a big house. He shook himself and focused on his escape. He couldn't deal with memories in this house where his mother and father slept. He had to get away.

Brad snuck down the stairs and helped himself to boxes of juice, tins of beans, luncheon meat, and a frozen loaf of brown bread, honey and a box of matches.

Upstairs he packed quietly; knife, hatchet, compass, map. He filled his canteen with cold water. Two problems haunted him as he worked. What about his paper route? What about his mother?

School. He didn't want to be there, not when Buckles told the kids, not when his friends found out.

He pulled a piece of paper out of his three-ring binder and grabbed a blue ballpoint pen.

Dear Mom and Dad,

I've gone away. Mrs. Buckholz told me about Killop. Is that why you left Saskatoon, too? Phone the Journal *and tell them I quit.*

Love, Bradley.

He erased the word love, stared at the paper, then scrunched it into a ball and tossed it into the trash. He took a clean sheet.

Mom,

I've gone camping.

Love, Brad.

He stretched out on the quilt in his hiking clothes. He slept, dreaming again of running down corridors, falling out of spacecraft windows. He woke gasping for breath.

At dawn he delivered papers, his sleeping bag and knapsack strapped to his bike. He rode out of town before anyone was up. Old Drum's dog kept him company until he reached the highway.

18. ALONE

BRAD'S LUNGS SCREAMED as he cycled. Ground fog a foot deep covered the prairie, cutting the bottom off trees, standing cattle, monster hay bales and deserted tractors. His fingers tingled with cold as he gripped the handlebars. The concrete pain of exerting himself helped.

By the time he pulled into Peebles' lane he was ready to drop.

He hid his bike behind a thick bank of carragana bushes, tossed his gear over the fence and vaulted the gate. Wisps of departing fog shrouded the silent woods. A hint of morning sun warmed his face. Brad pulled on his knapsack, strapped it to his hips and jogged past the empty country house to the ravine, across the Scout bridge where the fog lingered dense as cotton batting, up the slope on the other side to a group of pines and birches. He turned and surveyed the approach.

From the front of a lean-to built here he could see the road leading to the Peebles'. If any one came, he could put out the camp fire and take off for the back of the property. A quarter of a section, half-mile by half-mile, 160 acres of gray wooded soil. He knew about this. His mom had explained it when she had taken him with her to visit farms she was about to list for sale last year, before his dad had come home. Back when life was simple.

A disturbed squirrel chattered in the nearest pine. Two crows caterwauled from the creek. Brad set to work with hatchet and saw.

"I know, I know, you've had the whole place to yourselves for ages. It won't be long now until the human beings come back. Matt said they were coming on the long weekend. I won't bother you, okay." *I need to figure things out,* he continued, talking to himself. *I can't go around beating people up, just because my dad's some kind of weirdo. Becoming a bully like Buckles is no answer.*

He selected two sturdy birches about six feet apart. He found a three-inch poplar and cut an eight-foot length, dug in his backpack for lashing ropes and bound the poplar to the birches at a height of five feet. Two saplings angled from the birch were strapped in place before he foraged for branches. The early buds, the pale green leaves were not plentiful. He relied heavily on diamond willow, dogwood and baby poplar.

Brad wiped sweat from his eyes with his work gloves, only to scrape his face with wild rose thorns. The sun was high in the sky by the time he threw himself on the thick bed of pinecone flakes the squirrel had left. Kenny would like this, but Kenny was in school. In school with Buckles and Buckles had promised to tell the kids. Brad pulled his knees to his chest and rested his head on his arms. *How do you think your way out of this one, Brad?*

His stomach rumbled, reminding him of how hungry he was, so he postponed serious thought and collected deadfall twigs, branches and the chunks from the ends of his lean-to logs, balancing his cooking pot on a wire grate he had invented. Brad lit a fire, surrounding it with rocks, keeping his canteen nearby in case of wild fire. Fire could be such a friend, friend and foe at the same time. Poor old Sawdust Johnny.

He wolfed down beans, canned meat and bread. At the creek he washed the dishes, the pot and packed them away in his kit. No sense tempting wild animals. He wiped his hands on his shirt, glanced at his watch. The kids would be going to gym. Kenny's dad would be running them through their paces. Mrs. Peebles would be teaching social studies. His mom would be wondering where he was.

He didn't want to hurt her. He just wanted to know how to handle this. First, the fire and Sawdust Johnny's death. No matter what happened to him, Brad would never forget that dead ugly foot sticking out from under the sheet. His throat still tightened thinking of it. Then, Buckles and the bingo game. He could hear Buckles' voice, snide as ever, joyful, 'yur dad's sick all right, he's been in jail, he's ...' Brad couldn't go any further, thinking was making him dizzy, making his head feel like a football spinning out of control. He leapt up.

Brad stamped out the fire, tied his hiking boots tightly, making sure the laces were tucked in so he wouldn't trip. Alone in the bush you have to be careful, he said to himself. Grant Traynor had taught him that.

Grant Traynor had taught them lots of safety precautions, lots of neat stuff, taken them places. He was a pretty good Scout leader, even if he was flaky and stupid about cars. The guy really thrived on kids and confusion. Maybe he should ask Mr. Traynor to help him control his temper. It flared like flash fires!

Brad followed the path to the back of the farm. A few early strawberry plants dotted the way with tiny white blossoms. The smell of thawing ground frost, buds and muskeg made the air as rich as the sip of wine he had been allowed at Christmas dinner.

Too bad about the Science Fair, all that work and he wouldn't be there for it. Entries were due tonight. He couldn't make it, not tonight, maybe never. His teeth chattered. He pulled his jacket tight around him.

The northern woods were silent except for a few chickadees scolding from a thicket. Above Brad's head the giant poplars whispered their secrets to the rising chill wind, their fresh new leaves glowing, creating a translucent green canopy. New growth was everywhere. A distant tractor ploughed the barely thawed ground. A silent hawk, its wings blocking the sun, soared on a current of air, watching for prey. Brad walked on, each step taking him farther away from Camden, deeper into the dark woods where pines and thick floor cover hushed even the birds. The brooding forest left Brad breathless. He was used to being alone, so what frightened him? Was it the silence or the strange pain that filled his chest, a pain that slowed his footsteps, strained each muscle?

Ahead sunlight filled a clearing. He headed toward it, each footfall muffled by the thick bed of moss and pinecone flakes. A mule deer, two, three browsed in the pasture.

Brad froze in his tracks. The wind caressed his face. With the breeze blowing his way the deer would not smell him. Their donkey-like ears waved, turning like flowers searching for the sun's rays. They were alert to sounds, to danger. How beautiful they were, their tawny coats flooded with sun, their tails flipping, showing white rumps. They moved from clump to clump of alfalfa, barley, sedge, pawing the heaved uneven ground. What a gentle way to live, browsing, moving plant to plant. But always the fear, the consciousness of danger.

The wind shifted, the first deer's head sprang up, her large eyes resting on Brad, eyes filled with suspicion, wonder. What was this?

Curious, she's curious, like me. Suddenly all the deer leaped for the fence line. A fawn, all spots and skinny legs, and hidden until now by her mother's body, followed. They disappeared into a grove of willow.

Brad straightened, eased muscles sore from holding still. That's when he saw her, the deer that had stood closest to him—he could tell, one of her ears had a gouge, an old wound perhaps—the doe had come back to watch him, stepping lightly on the stubble in the field, picking her way, trying to look as if she was eating, but watching him.

An early fly lit on Brad's cheek, he wiggled his nose to dislodge it. It buzzed his eye. He swept it off. The deer bounced away like a rubber ball, back hooves landing where front hooves had landed. She cleared the fence easily and was gone.

Brad strolled into the pasture and across to the back of the Peebles' land, where the yellow and black "No Trespassing, No Hunting" signs hung. He leaned on the fence, staring at distant cows.

The deer were safe here. They were protected. They could munch on forage crops or leaves, or bark, depending on the season. They moved fast when they needed to. They were beautiful creatures. *If deer can live with their enemies and the dangers that surround them, if they can browse here and there, be with other deer or on their own, if deer can do all that, can human beings? Can I?*

The deer had come back to check him out, just the way curiosity drove Brad to check things out. He took a different path back to the lean-to as the sun crowded the treetops to the west. He bent and rescued a newly fallen young birch, the right size for a staff, and strode across the field and into the woods. He whistled a few bars of "Venus" from Holst's *The Planets* as he moved through the undergrowth; he flicked spider webs away and jumped over a fallen tree and branches. *I bet they have to clear the path of deadfall every spring,* he thought. *Even when no human is present, the woods go on living, growing, changing, dying.* He could understand that crazy Texan blabbermouth, Jessica, wanting to be an earth scientist. Too bad he only had one life. He'd like to know about plants and trees and soils, too.

You can't know it all, Brad, a small voice inside said, a voice like his mother's.

But I can know more. I want to learn more, that's who I am.

He relit the fire, stretched out on his sleeping bag and dozed off. The squirrel watched from a safe distance.

For supper Brad ate more beans, canned meat, juice, and toast with honey for dessert. He put on another sweater as the sun, having washed the sky with brilliant reddish gold and coated the undersides of clouds with lilac and pink, sank behind the black silhouettes of trees. Dark clouds gathered in the north.

Brad piled branches, broken or chopped in short chunks, close by his side. His flashlight and canteen rested on a rock by his pillow. He stared into the flames, entranced by their dancing, the riot of colors, reminiscent of the sunset.

He poked a stick into the flames and watched as it was consumed by the fire. The heat flushed his face, sparks flitted in the updraft like fireflies and the branches crackled and hissed.

Brad envied the stick, eaten by flames, totally devoured. Maybe that was the answer for him, too. Just disappear forever. He shivered and pulled his coat collar higher. Part of him felt dead like the stick. If he disappeared, he wouldn't have to face his friends or his father. He wouldn't have to deal with the pain. What if his dad's problem was hereditary? What had his dad done? Those boys had trusted him, he was their teacher. He couldn't force himself to think about the details. Brad felt dirty all over, slimy. The blackness from inside had spread through his bloodstream and was coating his brain and covering his skin. It smelt of musty graves and carrion. If he disappeared forever into that dark universe, then everyone else could get on with their lives. Desmond and Una would move to the city. The kids would forget about him and life would go on. And he would have all the room in the world—or in heaven. Did you go to heaven, if there was one, if you took your own life? Oh you can't get to heaven, that's what the song said. A silly song that had bad memories for him. Memories he had wanted to explore. If he stayed.

He could leave tonight. He had a sharp knife. He had fire. Not far away was a bottomless lake.

The coyotes at the back of the place set up a yip-yipping chorus. The moon came out from behind a cloud. The darkness inside receded. The universe righted itself.

Taking your own life took a lot of work, especially in Canada. There weren't guns lying around everywhere. He'd never seen a gun in his whole life. You had to choose the right time, place and method. Kids who really did that must be in pain for a long time, must have forgotten how to see both sides of things, must have forgotten how to think about options.

Suddenly he was glad he was who he was. Brad Greaves didn't solve things that way. He unwrapped a chocolate bar and wolfed it down.

He glanced up, asking the Pole Star for the courage to do the remembering he had to do, the strength to stay alive and to do the planning he had to do. If he had been a different kind of kid, maybe like Kenny or Lane, he might have been able to get help with this. Brad shook his head and licked his lips, they were so dry. But I'm not like Kenny or Lane, I'm not like any of the other kids in my troop. I'm me. I have to do things my way. I have to sit here and figure life out for myself. He began scraping the bark off the birch sapling, revealing the actual wood, the creamy white wood, raw and smooth as bone. Several knots gave him trouble. The evening woods behind him smelled musty, like closets or that old teddy-bear slipper.

He must have been five or six when it happened, for his body was short and stocky, straw-colored bangs hanging over his eyes. He was in an old house with large rooms and high ceilings. The wallpaper had green ferns and flowers. He was standing in a doorway wiping sleep from his eyes. Music played on a stereo turntable, not a CD, not a modern audio system like Greaves had now, a cheaper one. Debussy or Fauré played softly. It was a big house with wood floors and miles of hallways, stairs with bannisters to slide down. Fruit trees in a big yard, and an old woman with white hair and tiny whiskers sprouting on her chin living in the house next door, a woman who made chocolate chip cookies and read him picture books. That must have been Great Aunt Belle?

The fire burned higher. The knife slid down the staff, a pile of curled shavings grew by his knee. A wave of dizziness washed over Brad as the memory continued.

Loud singing came from the flagstone patio beyond the grand piano, the organ and the stacks of student books, theory lessons, sheet music, piles of concertos and ballads his daddy played. Spread on the table were magazines for waiting students: Archie *comics,* Sports Illustrated, Body Building at Home. *Photo features of young people playing on beaches with palm trees waving overhead, young men wrestling.*

The smell of his father's after-shave was strongest here, in the music room. His father laughing at him, poking him in the tummy with a long bony finger. "A Clark through and through, built like a brick wall. Not like me. Maybe your mother found you in the bushes, Bradley." He tossed fine black hair out of his bulgy blue eyes, which looked like they might fall out in a moment of anger and roll across the floor, glaring at little Brad. The doorbell would ring and his father's student would enter, receive a smile, a hand on the shoulder. Brad would have to leave, be quiet as a mouse.

In this particular memory the boy shuddered, standing by the coffee table with its clutter of shiny photos, the boy shuddered listening to the splashes and the loud voices singing. His feet were cold, he had forgotten his teddy-bear slippers and his blue striped bathrobe and gone to his mother's room hoping to find her and recover from the nightmare, the dinosaur that chased him, a Tyrannosaurus rex. His mother had not been in her room so he had come downstairs following the sounds.

The walking stick was finished. The layers of outer and inner bark lay in tiny mountains on the ground. He had peeled, scraped and sliced until the real wood was revealed. Brad lay the gleaming staff beside him on the grass. He cracked his knuckles one by one, the snapping of his bones reassuring him. He threw two more logs on the fire and wrapped his hands around his knees, hugging them tightly. The stars appearing slowly above, and the roaring flames gave him courage to return to the memory. This was hard work, harder than fractions or exams. Maybe he should forget it, let the past sink like a stone in the brook that gurgled nearby.

One glowing chunk of poplar rolled off the fire. Brad prodded it back in, shoved it to the heart of the orange coals. Flames scorched the end of his fire stick, curled his nostrils. He returned to his story.

Small bare feet padding over shiny slippery hardwood floors and bushy scatter mats to the open patio doors where billows of steam rose above a hot tub.

Here it was then, the hot tub that he remembered, that made him feel like he had been a bad boy for a long time. Brad pushed on.

His father sat on the side of the spa, feet and calves in water. The tub was full of big boys, music students, the ones with talent, the ones who got cookies and milk and special help.

You can't get to heaven in new blue jeans
'Cause all the angels will split their seams
You can't get to heaven …

The kids were splashing each other, calling each other names. Their voices sounded too loud, their faces were flushed. His daddy sat on the edge of the tub directing like an orchestra conductor. Half hidden in steam, his hands waved above the crowd. He brushed water from the cheek of the dark-haired boy beside him, gave him a hug and whispered in his ear. The boy froze and pulled away. Daddy's eyes were glazed, his face red, the muscles in his neck working fiercely. Something was wrong. He looked dizzy, sick. Little Bradley ran to him. "Daddy, daddy."

"What are you doing here?" One boy pointed. "Did you wet the bed? Are you looking for your mommy?" All the boys roared. One slim boy scooped water out of the tub and splashed him. "Go change your jammies, naughty boy." No one looked happy. This was not a happy party, not a happy party at all. One boy slid out of the tub and ran shivering to the house.

Above the crowd and through the mist his father stared at little Bradley as if he had never seen him before, as if he were a stranger.

Those bulgy eyes with long black lashes dripping scanned Brad's shaking body, taking in the bare feet, the wrinkled airplane pjs, stopped at his face. The two of them, man and boy, said nothing but their eyes held. The father's eyelids drooped, hooding a dark look, and his body slipped into the water to the neck. "Go back to bed, you bad boy. Forget this ever happened. It's none of your business." The shouted command was one the boy had never heard before. "If you tell, I'll never forgive you."

He mounted the stairs. There were still thirteen and the second one creaked. The little boy lay in his bed trying to get back to sleep. He heard the boys leave, his mother come back. She tiptoed in and bent over him. He turned his head and scrunched his eyes shut as if asleep. "I must never tell, I must never tell. What must I never tell?" He slept heavily. In the morning he went to school and memorized his numbers. He read all the books in the library about dinosaurs, even the ones for Third Graders, until he knew enough, until he knew there was nothing to fear from dinosaurs. He never got up in the night again.

Shortly after that the police car had come and his father had gone away. His mother had cried, waterlogged her geraniums, and given away her ferns. The old woman next door had yelled, had slammed a door. His mother cried and held him for a little while, just a little while. Una May and Bradley had moved to Saskatoon. Your daddy's sick, is all she said. He can't come home. You have to be the man of the house now.

"Poor dumb little kid, you weren't a bad boy, you were scared." Brad spoke to the silent poplars. He wished he could hug that little boy in bare feet, little Bradley with his missing teddy-bear slippers, hold him and tell him he had been a good boy, tell him it was going to be all right. Brad wrapped his arms around his knees and rocked by the fire, rocked gently back and forth, back and forth, until he felt better.

Brad filled his cooking pot with water, sliced three pieces of bread and found a perfect toasting spot. He watched as the bread changed color and the familiar smell of toast rose. A coyote howled in the distance.

"You wouldn't like toast anyway," Brad said aloud. "Go hunt rabbit." His voice echoing off the cliff comforted him. He didn't feel so alone, not with squirrels and deer and dumb old coyotes lurking by the creek.

He stirred five teaspoons of hot chocolate into his mug of boiling water, munched on toast and honey and leaned against a pine tree. He rubbed sticky fingers along the seams of his jeans, feeling the rough fabric. Here, at Peebles' place everything he touched, heard, smelt, tasted seemed sharper, clearer. Maybe he could stay out here forever, do chores for his keep, take correspondence courses and be a hermit and live with the stars. Brad took out his grandfather's binoculars, his constellation map from his shirt pocket, and a stub of a pencil, spread it out on the ground. He turned the flashlight on to check the old maps, then he returned the light to his belt.

The Little Dipper was above and to his right in the northwest sky. The Pole Star glimmered. On the same level but more westerly was Capella, brightest star in Auriga the Charioteer steering his way across the heavens. *How do I steer my way?* Brad asked himself. Taurus the Bull hung below that, sharing one star with the Charioteer. Ursa Major, the Big Dipper, was high in the sky. By training the binoculars between the Big Dipper and Gemini he could pick up the Lynx faintly.

Brad put down the binoculars, stuffed his pencil and log book in his shirt pocket, lay on his back and let the whole of the night sky stretch above him.

A bull bellowed. Another bull, closer, probably on the next farm, answered. A watch-dog yapped, a branch in the fire snapped. Otherwise the night was still, the sky a dome of flickering lights, some bright, some faint, some looking blue like Mars, or orange like Venus, others cold and distant as other galaxies. Brad traced the constellations with his fingers; Perseus, Cassiopea, Cepheus, Drago. It was comfortable to name the stars, the planets, to know where each one was, where each one fit, to study the patterns. Someone like him, maybe hundreds of kids like him, had lain on the ground beside campfires watching stars, naming constellations—for centuries, for aeons.

A shooting star crossed the sky. Brad's head moved with it. *I belong in the universe. I belong to all of history. It's going home, it's living day-to-day that's hard. It's finding a place for me.*

Did I think it was my fault that my father went away, that he wouldn't touch me? Was I trying to be responsible for something I didn't do. Old Drum is right, there is random good, random evil. Brad tossed another log on the fire. *I sound like Lane, trying to figure people out.* He stood and stretched, gripped the new Scout staff firmly in his right hand. *I'm just a kid, for crying out loud.*

The storm in the north had turned the bottom half of the night sky into a rolling, boiling cloud mass. The cold wind sent sparks from the fire soaring high in the air. Brad pulled his ski jacket on. Lightning flashed. Thunder shook the forest floor. Brad timed the gap between crashes. The storm was only three miles away.

Suddenly, stuck between the friendly campfire and the fearsome bolts of lightning in the angry sky, Brad heard a slow scream, more like a loud moan. It went on for a minute before he realized it was himself, crying out, crying out like one of those coyotes, crying out like a wounded animal. He was not little Bradley any more, he was a grown boy who had to howl, maybe at the storm, maybe at life itself. The sound filled the air and Brad knew at that moment that he really was here—on the Earth, this startling planet, and he was glad. The sounds had left his body quivering, tired out. *How do I live with the good and the bad, the right and the wrong, all the feelings that roll over me like those storm clouds rolling overhead?*

Don't ask so many questions, his mother's voice reminded him. *Don't fret yourself so.*

The first few hailstones clattered to the ground, danced into the fire, ricocheted off the cooking pot and the rocks, plopping on the wet earth. Some were as big as marbles. Brad's new Scout staff fell to the ground and rolled away.

What am I going to do? Brad asked the melting hailstones. He reached for a few that had landed just outside his lean-to, popped one in his mouth, let it melt on his tongue. It tasted like glaciers and snow, cold and gritty.

Brad drew a line in the dirt with a thin willow twig. He put a big C for Camden on the right side, and a big ? on the left side.

In Camden he had a father who had been to jail, kids at school who knew about it, a history of losing his temper, and a lot of people upset with him.

Out here he had a knapsack full of stuff and fifty dollars from his paper collections. He could run away like that abused English kid had and cycle across Canada, maybe find a job where people didn't know how old he was. Or he could move to the city, go see the Child Welfare people and say he was homeless. They would check up on him. That would hurt his mom.

On the other hand—without thinking his fingers moved back to the Camden side of the scratched score card—on the other hand he had Scouts, and his mom, and school in Camden. Even if he and the other kids bitched about some of the teachers, Brad liked it most of the time. If he left, he wouldn't get to go to school—or get Scout badges or enter Science Fairs.

What about Kenny and Lane? He'd miss them, and if he left he wouldn't dare come back, not after the lesson they'd taught him on the sleigh ride, about keeping friends. Besides he'd promised Kenny that they'd go to the Scout Jamboree together. Mr. Drum wanted him to make little power lines for his great train setup.

Running away wouldn't solve anything. He'd have to start all over again somewhere else. Living outdoors would be fine in the summer, but tough all year round. Someday perhaps, but he'd need better equipment and maybe some friends along, now that he knew what friends were for.

Too bad about the Fair. He'd had so much fun doing the projects, taxing himself to the limit building the telescope. He could live off that for awhile. Winning wasn't everything, Mr. Traynor was right about that. Brad hadn't believed him when he'd said it. He did now.

The kids at school would give him a tough time, but most of his friends would be okay. Especially after a couple of days. His dad had had problems but Brad didn't, except for his temper, and he was working on that.

Brad scraped the line in the dirt, the big C and ? away with his scuffed sneaker. Let's face it; he didn't want to run away, he didn't want to leave.

He leaned against the back of his shelter, the bark digging into his skin. *I have to go back. Tough luck, Brad, you've got a dad who's been to jail. Was he in hospital, too, or was that part lies?*

An elk bugled in the bush. Brad stuck his head out and looked around. The storm had passed nearly as fast as it had come; the fire was spluttering, dying. He built it up high, rubbed his hands together, warming them in the flames, smelling the hair on the back of his hands singe. He poked a stick into the hottest part of the fire, watched it burn, turn from brown to orange to red. He lifted an empty, red-hot tin can out of the fire with his stick and dropped it on the wet earth. It sizzled as it cooled.

Now he would stomp on it, take it with him, because a good camper never left garbage behind. The can had gone through the fire, its label and what was left of its contents had been burned away. In some ways he had gone through the fire too.

Brad was exhausted. The North Star winked at him as the last of the storm clouds dissipated. He curled up at the front of his shelter, where he could watch the night sky and the fire at the same time. Brad's eyes closed, popped open and closed again. He slept.

He dreamt of the spaceship again. Only this time there were two of them linked together—one had people on board, familiar looking people, the other was empty and still. He kept wandering back and forth between the two.

A car horn woke him. Headlights shone on the hill, moved down Peebles' lane, lit up the skinny track to the creek.

"Brad, Brad, are you down there?" Lane shouted from the van window.

"Buffalo biscuits!" Kenny exploded from the back door and hurtled towards Brad's fire. "Did you have us scared, you fig newton, numbnuts." He threw himself on top of Brad.

"We would have come sooner but we took your entries to the fair grounds." Lane sauntered up the slope and stood hands on hips staring down at the two boys rolling on the ground.

"What?"

"Hey, we figured you wanted to win. You like competing

so much." Kenny tossed a green branch on the flame. Sparks rose like fire crackers.

"You've got to come back with us."

"But."

"Are you going to keep talking in monosyllables?" Lane laughed.

"But, my dad."

"Yeah, we heard, your dad's been in jail," Kenny said. "What a bummer."

"Shut up, Kenny." Grant Traynor muffled his son's face in the sleeve of a sweater with arms long enough for a giant sloth. "Brad's dad has had a problem. He's in therapy."

Grant's woolly sleeve enfolded Brad. "All of us have something to put up with. My mom was an alcoholic when I was your age. She couldn't face the truth for years." Caught in Mr. Traynor's bear hug, Brad let unasked-for tears soak into the Scoutmaster's bushy sweater. He was so glad to see them he didn't know what to say. He stammered.

"But my dad, it's not the same thing …" he pulled away.

"I know. This isn't easy for any of us," Mr. Traynor said. "We've been at your house. Desmond didn't want to talk about it at first. He says it happened a long time ago. He says he's cured." Grant looked upset, but not with Brad. "You aren't your father, Brad." Grant handed Brad a giant cowboy hankie to wipe the smoke, the tears from his face.

"Your mom wants you to come home, Brad." Lane's eyes glinted in the firelight. "She says she wanted to tell you but …"

"My dad …"

"He's gone to the city for his therapy session, and to play at El Rancho. He hurried away. Seems he has rented an apartment close to his work. Says commuting is too hard. Your mother isn't sure what to do," Mr. Traynor sighed. It sounded typical. Brad wasn't sure he was ready for the next step.

Grant Traynor wiped his big hands on his baggy pants. He ambled down to the creek with a tin pail. It clanged against his leg as he walked.

For a second Brad wanted to run after him—like a little boy—and take his hand and hold tightly to it. But he knew he wasn't a little boy anymore.

"So are you coming with us?" Kenny jumped on Brad's back.

Brad dumped Kenny on the ground and began stamping out the fire. Grant came puffing up the slope with a bucket of water from the creek. The ashes sizzled and spluttered in the fire pit.

"You'd already decided to come back, hadn't you?" Lane said as they climbed the hill to rescue his bike.

Brad nodded. He looked into her eyes and saw a welcome. He heaved a big sigh.

"How'd you know where to find me?" He tossed the birch staff into the back of the van with his bike and other gear. He had a small can of varethane in his workshop that would make the wood glow.

"Old Drum said he saw you heading this way."

"He's a friend of mine, " Brad grinned in the dark as they climbed into the back seat. "He's got this great train set in his basement he and his wife Florence used to play with together. Now I help. I was thinking of designing an automatic starter for his control tower."

Lane smirked at Kenny and her dad. "Sounds like Brad."

19. You Can't Have Everything

☆

ALL THE LIGHTS were blazing in Brad's house when the Traynors' van pulled in the driveway. Brad's mom must have been standing behind the curtains in the music room because she emerged from the door in a matter of seconds. Brad hopped down and ran toward her.

Una May Greaves wrapped her arms around her son. Her gray hair brushed his cheek. "You're home." She didn't know what to do with her body, and Brad felt awkward, too. He broke away from the embrace first, to help lift his bicycle out of the back of the van.

"Right where we thought he'd be." Grant patted Brad's mother's arm as if she were a injured child on the playground.

Kenny and Lane sat in the back seat like two obedient puppies.

"We'll pick you up at nine o'clock sharp." Grant hugged Brad, holding him in a warm woolly bear hug. The giant sloth sweater enfolded him in a mat of after-shave and man smell. "You had us scared."

"We thought you might get suicidal," Kenny said. "You were pretty upset."

"Shut up, Kenny," Lane said.

"Right."

"I'm not the type," Brad said.

"I'm glad." Lane leaned forward so she could see past Kenny. "I didn't think you were."

"Good luck tomorrow," Grant Traynor said.

Brad turned to go into the house.

"Thanks," Brad's mom said. "Thanks so much. If Des was here, he'd add his thanks, too."

"The kids at school know your dad was in jail, Brad," Grant whispered. "They don't know everything. Rory only told them that. Someone reminded him that his dad was still in jail and the fun went out of it."

"Come on, Dad," Lane said. "Brad doesn't need all the details. He's a big boy, he can work things out for himself."

Brad grinned at her. Trust Lane to put her finger on the situation. They should fire the school counsellor and give her the job. It was like a sixth sense, and he was glad she had it. He had the strangest urge to clamber into the van and kiss her. He winked instead. He really hadn't figured out how to smooch. He'd have to learn. He laughed as he waved goodbye, shouted parting shots at Kenny. "Tomorrow, weasel."

"Wombat."

"Whirlybird."

"What are you laughing at?" Lane hollered over the roar of the engine.

"Nothing." But he had been laughing at something, he'd been laughing about going to the library and asking for a book about love, about hugging and kissing. He couldn't see himself asking the librarian for help with that. Maybe he'd watch movies, TV, the high school kids, and Grant and Anna Traynor.

"Cocoa, Brad?" his mom asked. She looked nervously around the kitchen as if she'd forgotten where everything was.

"No, thanks, I'm pooped. Papers in the morning, the Spring Fair."

"I found the other note, the one in the wastebasket. I'm sorry."

Brad cracked his knuckles, looked away.

"Desmond's in therapy. He paid a high price. We all did. I hated the moving, losing my roots, but they were an unforgiving lot. A small town is like that, a small town never forgets. Never forgives, either. Your dad isn't a bad man, Brad. He's made a few mistakes, but he's not really bad, believe me."

"Buckles' mom knows you. She was in your Sunday School class."

"I've seen her places, but I avoided her. I thought we could run away. I thought we could hide."

"It doesn't work, Mom. I ought to know." He picked up his knapsack, bent and pecked her cheek. "I'm going to bed."

A look of relief flooded her face, her lips quivered.

"I'll stay up for a while. Your dad is staying in the city overnight. He wants us to move to the city, you know. He's rented an apartment. He says it would be safer there. That no one would know about his past. He was so worried about you when he left."

Brad nodded. Right, Mom. Hiding from the truth can get to be a habit.

☆

The Agricom resounded with the voices of participants,

judges, parents, and sponsoring businesses; hawkers with coffee, muffins, cinnamon buns; patrolling security guards and electrical crews stringing last minute lights, microphones and loud speakers. Brad ran from one booth to the next ensuring that his inventions, experiments, games and projects were set up and running.

A crowd of children had lined up to play his stargazers video game. Two senior high boys were poking around his telescope.

"Did you build this, kid?" The tall one with thick glasses asked. "How long did it take?"

As he explained, blushing with pride, his stomach whirled like a helicopter blade. His hands kept moving as he talked, waving as he described the process. If he didn't know better he'd say he was nervous.

Everything he'd done for the last eight months was on display. He didn't feel like a cool kid at all. He wanted to win so badly he could taste it. He wanted his picture in the paper. Beside his mother, beside his mother.

Kenny strolled up, cool as a cucumber. "Judging starts soon. Are you ready?"

"How come you're so relaxed?"

"I've worried myself here. It's too late now, bratwurst."

"Kenny Bunkport, if it hadn't been for you guys, I'd still be out at Peebles'."

"Hey, I wasn't going to do this without you. Next year we can enter the Provincial Science Fair. If you are still here, that is. If you haven't decided that this is geeky."

"The judges are circulating." Lane came up behind the two boys and gave them a double hug. "Let's go for muffins. I can't stand the tension and Brad looks like he's going to have a conniption fit."

As they wandered around trying to find a place without a lineup, they passed the Yamaha piano booth. Brad's dad was talking to a man in a bright blue blazer and white flannels.

"There's your dad," Kenny said.

"Brilliant observation," Lane quipped.

"It's not like he's a crook," Kenny added. "He makes me nervous, though. He's kind of strange."

"Shut up, Kenny," Lane said.

"Shut up, Kenny."

"Right."

"I'll be right back," Brad said. His father had come.

His insides were in knots as he walked over to where his dad was playing. His ears burned. He put his hand on the shiny lid of the grand piano and cleared his throat.

His father kept playing but his eyes focused on Brad. His face looked pinched, his lips thin. He played a set of chords and dropped his hands in his lap.

"Dad, I want to say something."

His father lifted his right hand and gripped the piano. His mouth opened as if to speak.

"Before you say anything, I have to say something." Brad could hear the giant fans on the ceiling. "I was not a bad boy. I did not tell on you."

"I know."

"You should have told me the truth. I hate all this family secret business. It doesn't work. Did Mom tell you about Rory Buckholz? What a heck of a way to find out."

"I didn't want you to know."

"I'm your son, for crying out loud. You shouldn't lie to your kids."

"We can move."

"Moving isn't the answer. Mom and I like it here."

☆ 184 ☆

"It's not what you think. Kids shouldn't talk like this to their parents. Kids should respect their elders." His father's voice was rising. He was turning the conversation around. "Nobody ever listens to my side of the story."

"You've been in jail, Dad. You told me it was a hospital. That's lying. You told me I was bad. I wasn't bad. I was just a little kid with a nightmare. You've turned my whole life into a nightmare. I want it to stop. I want it to stop now." Brad could feel the anger rushing through his blood stream, threatening to burst through his fists. He clutched the top of the piano.

His father was speaking. "... things were blown all out of proportion. The second time was just a little lapse. The doctor says I'm making real progress. Better than all those criminals. Better than those stupid people in That Place."

Brad drew a breath. Had his father heard anything he had said? He let go of the piano slowly and pushed his hands into his pockets. He started to back away from the piano.

"Brad, I care. I really do." His father's voice was low and careful and only loud enough for Brad to hear. "I just have trouble saying it. Listen to the music. It's in the music."

A group of people approached the Yamaha booth and his dad looked away, pressed his fingers along the creases in his trousers, pushed his hair out of his eyes and began to play dance tunes.

Kenny and Lane had found a booth that sold orange juice and home-made muffins. Brad joined them. He didn't say anything for a few minutes. He was going though the past scene in his mind. He felt better. He had said what he had to say. Whether it did any good or not only time would tell.

The three friends sat eating and drinking, watching the funny people, all different sizes and shapes, moving from stall to table.

"Everyone's going in circles." Brad wiped butter from his chin. "Orbiting like rocks in the rings of Saturn."

"You have planets on the brain," Kenny teased.

"It's better than dwelling on problems he can't solve," Lane said.

Brad nodded. He glanced across the table at Lane Traynor and looking straight into her eyes, nodded again. She smiled and he felt as if her dancing eyes were brighter than his favorite stars.

A gust of wind blew her bangs into her eyes and brought drifting snow through the open doors. "Oh, no." Lane spread her hands in a gesture of annoyance. "More walks to shovel."

"I'm sick of snow." Kenny pushed through the crowds to the auditorium with its hundreds of ugly battleship-gray folding chairs in stark rows. Primary kids played tag up and down the aisles. The judges arrived in groups of two with clip boards and stacks of entry forms. They were a motley crew, the ones from the city trying to look sophisticated with jackets and ties or dresses. The high school teachers and business leaders from town looked casual in a ritzy way, neat creases in their cords or brand names on their jeans or sportswear. Mrs. Peebles' hair was tied in a bun, her plum shoes matching her suit. Brad cracked his knuckles over and over until Lane glared at him.

The mayor spoke first, thanking all the sponsors, the townsfolk, and the participants, all five hundred and twenty-three of them.

Next, the principal of the composite high school spoke,

and the president of the Kiwanis. Brad tapped his feet and estimated the dimensions of the room, wondered if they'd ever thought of issuing roller-blades to the security staff.

Grant joined them. Anna Traynor and Buddy Beaver in his hot costume were manning the Forestry booth in the annex of the Agricom. "She'd like to be here with us, but you know how it goes, you can't have everything."

Finally Mrs. Peebles, the honorary chair of the Fair and one of the judges, rose.

"It gives me a great deal of pleasure to announce the winners of the Fair for this year. Would they please come forward to accept their ribbons, and thanks to the Kiwanis club, their prize money.

"In the area of fine arts, first prize goes to ..." Brad started cracking his knuckles again as the award winners for pottery, weaving, painting, sculpture, photography, woodwork and knitting went forward.

"On the Science side we have an unusual circumstance. Two boys have won the majority of the prizes."

Brad glanced over at Kenny who blushed.

"They may get tired of running up to the stage and back, so I will ask Kenny Traynor, our last year's top winner, and Brad Greaves to join me on the stage. Between the two of them they have submitted twenty first and twelve second-prize entries for a total of thirty-two. What an grand acheivement! Topping the charts is Brad Greaves, with a score of 14 first-place ribbons, and four second-place, and Kenny with a score of six first places and eight seconds.

"Top award for the Scientist of the Year goes to Bradley Greaves of Camden, with his Stargazers Video Game, chosen by the judges as the most innovative project submitted."

Brad's face flushed as the audience applauded and the

President of the Chamber of Commerce presented the trophy. His eyes swept the crowd. Old Drum stood near the front clapping like crazy. Lane and Grant Traynor grinned and cheered. At the far side his mom and dad stood together. The other Scouts waved. Matt Peebles threw a paper cup in the air. Mrs. Peebles frowned.

Brad grinned as the local paper's sole photographer-reporter took a picture, the flashing bulb making dots appear behind his eyelids. Where was the city paper, the reporter and the photographer?

They finished the presentations of individual awards for each and every entry: electronic, electrical, physical, earth science, biological, mathematical, and astronomical. Here was where Brad excelled. He was surprised that his telescope, his beloved telescope, hadn't won the judge's honor prize. He'd won with the silly video game, invented on his computer in three days. Life didn't always make sense.

"We invite everyone to wander around and check out the wonderful array of entries, talk to the participants and winners, acquaint yourselves with their work." Mrs. Peebles shook Brad's hand and whispered, "If you ever need to talk about things, you know, private things that you have to work through, I'll be glad to help. "

Brad didn't say anything. What could he say? That he was all right, that he wanted to get on with building his life. He glanced around once more for the *Journal* photographer.

"Too bad about the blizzard, eh?" Grant Traynor came up beside him, slurping coffee, spilling some on his shirt, wiping it with his hand. "Anyone coming from the city would have second thoughts."

"I wanted that photo, the one like Kenny's last year. My dad liked that photo."

"He's playing up a storm over at the Yamaha booth. Let's go."

The two of them strolled through the mob. A small group had gathered around the piano. Old Drum was sitting on a spare piano bench. He waved at Brad. Brad's mom sat beside Desmond, straightening staff paper. She spotted Brad, nudged his dad who looked up and nodded at him, a small twitch rippling his cheek. He wiped his hands and mouth with a white handkerchief.

"For my next selection I'd like to play a new arrangement of a piece of music that ranks high in appeal in our family. Occasionally I manage time for serious composition in my busy schedule of playing in the city. Some of you have heard me at various hotels. I'm currently playing at El Rancho Downtown. It's not the Roy Thomson Hall, but you can't have everything."

The last row of the little crowd began to drift away.

"Get on with it, Dad," Brad pleaded in his head, "just get on with it."

Des tossed his hair, shook his hands above the keys, positioned his chair carefully. "It's a transcription for piano of Gustav Holst's *The Planets*. I'd like to play "Jupiter" for you, but especially for my son Bradley. He's a good boy and I'm very proud of him. He just won first prize." His dad's wide eyes blinked fiercely as he bobbed his head in Brad's direction and began to play.

His mother smiled at Brad and turned the pages, licking her lips in concentration.

The melody rolled effortlessly from the piano. The restless crowd stilled. Brad sighed and let the music flow over him like a shower after a dirty day's work. This is as good as it gets, then. You win the prize but the photographer doesn't show up. You build a telescope and spend months at it, and your computer game wins the judge's special notice. You find out just enough about your past to know it's not great, and then you have to live with it. His father was proud of him, that's what he had said—in words and in music. Brad leaned into the music like Desmond leaned over the piano, like his mother leaned into the page turning. The three of them caught for the moment in the same orbit.

The last chord sounded. Brad led the applause. He moved hesitantly toward his father, his throat sore, his big hands loose by his sides.

"Thanks, Dad. That was great." There was an awkward moment as the two of them stood facing each other, the nervous willowy man and the tall sturdy boy. Una May wavered between them. She grinned lopsidedly and her arms reached towards each of them as if they were plants that needed tending.

"I told you it would be fine, Desmond, Brad, I told you both."

Lane and Kenny raced up and pulled him away.

"How's it going, bratwurst?" Lane hollered, pulling on Brad's arm.

"Lane to the rescue," Kenny whispered. "How are you, superbrain?"

"Not bad, nutso."

"Let's go outside and throw snowballs," Kenny laughed.

"Look at the poor apple blossoms," Lane moaned. "Now they'll have to start all over again."

"Even apple trees can't win them all." Brad raised his eyes to the dull gray sky with snow sifting down like flour through a sieve, then turned his head towards his friends with a half-grin spreading across his face. "Did you guys know that above all that cloud-cover, behind the sunlight, the stars move, the planets orbit. We've a whole extravagant universe surrounding us with scads of room in it for all of us. The galaxies, stars and planets are up there whether we can see them or not. Did you know that?

Kenny and Lane shrugged their shoulders, arched their eyebrows. "Yes, Bradley, we know, we know." They pushed him in a snowbank and shoved wet flakes down his neck.

Brad didn't need to tell them how good it felt lying there on the earth, feeling its cold but solid strength beneath him, not to mention the warmth inside his chest where the darkness used to reside. He could hear his heart beating and knew he was really alive and he had everything to live for. He knew it would pass. But not yet. He felt completely at home in that instant. So he laughed, starting with a little ripple of chuckles and building to a giant rolling-around-on-the-ground laugh. Kenny and Lane joined him. It felt real good.